T0354537

MOMENTS IN TIME

A COLLECTION OF SHORT STORIES

BRIAN WILSON

Order this book online at www.trafford.com
or email orders@trafford.com

Most Trafford titles are also available at major online book retailers.

Printed in the United States of America.

ISBN: 978-1-4669-2624-0 (sc)
ISBN: 978-1-4669-2626-4 (hc)
ISBN: 978-1-4669-2625-7 (e)

Library of Congress Control Number: 2012906179

Trafford rev. 04/27/2012

 www.trafford.com

North America & international
toll-free: 1 888 232 4444 (USA & Canada)
phone: 250 383 6864 ♦ fax: 812 355 4082

TABLE OF CONTENTS

PHOTOGRAPHS

POEMS

DEDICATION

I WOULD LIKE to dedicate this book to the people of Christchurch who have endured too much for too long. Their resilience is admirable and an inspiration to all who are experiencing hard times. One earthquake of Richter scale of 5 or greater is an unwanted experience. Over a 5 Richter scale, one can expect books to fall off the shelves and food out of the pantry. The people of Christchurch have experienced over 30 of a Richter scale of 5 and greater in a period of 500 days, and 9000 over a Richter scale of 3. To go through each day not knowing when the next aftershock will come is daunting and unnerving.

FOREWORD

AS A LONG-TIME friend, I think I am more excited than Brian that he has finally taken steps to publishing these thirty short stories. Initially Brian read me two of his short stories (one to be published in his next book). An avid short story reader, I thought these were brilliant and must be published. Since then I have digested the contents between the covers which reinforces my first impressions.

The stories are not only told by Brian but are Brian, reflecting his witty sometime subtle sense of humour and play on words. They are naturally thought provoking. While these stories will be entertaining to most readers, the more discerning reader will be rewarded in discovery of the many subtleties. In these stories he mixes a wealth of New Zealand and overseas experiences with fiction. While mostly fiction, some stories are largely true, like those about the September and February earthquakes. As a Christchurch citizen, I too experienced these traumatic events and suffered loss. I commiserate with those who have endured so much more loss, like those who have lost family and friends from the February earthquake.

Another of the stories, "Weet-bix Mountain," I can assure you, is also in part true. Brian and I have tramped (hiked) this route many times together and the river crossing was our experience. However, Brian prefers to create his own characters and stories—often drawing from various experiences, so alas I do not feature.

"The Psychologist", might also to those who know Brian, appear to have some truthful elements. Brian has an MA (honours) in psychology and does like to observe people with his wicked desire of wanting to carry out experiments. I recall our teenage days at Easter Camp where Brian would get up to all sorts of mischief; not that I am altogether exonerated. The story "The Psychologist" is false, but it does provoke thought.

The many stories in "Moments In Time" reflect the types of experiences we all have in life, and these stories provide entertaining reading. As set out in Brian's poem "Moments in Time", these moments, and who we share them with, change as we journey through life from the cradle to the grave. In our earlier years as lads both Brian and I as good friends shared many similar moments, like Easter Camps and mountain tramps. Over the last three decades our moments have been different, as each has married and raised a family. We have also embarked on different careers; Brian's being more people focused while mine has been more problem focussed—at the cutting edge of medical technology.

Brian assures me that he has more stories to tell, so the reader will not be disappointed fearing that this is a one-off book. His last story brings some finality to the earthquake stories and a subtle ending to an enjoyable book of short stories.

David R Moore **M.Prof.Studs., Dip.Mgt., Cert.QA.**

ACKNOWLEDGEMENTS

PUTTING TOGETHER THIS book of short stories was a family effort. One son was involved in the creation of the book cover. Other family members contributed in the unenviable task of editing my work.

Special thanks to my wife Karen, and to other family members: Rachel, Andrew, Mark and Ben. I would also like to thank family and others, who have permitted me to use their photographs and tell some of their stories. Writing a Foreword and Biography can be a difficult task. In writing these sections, my friend David has been willing and enthusiastic, and more than generous in his appraisal. It is my hope that the reader will share the same sentiment and enjoy these stories.

"Alone we can do so little; together we can do so much,"

Helen Keller

The house shook and the pantry spewed out its contents

PREFACE

TUESDAY THE 22ND February 2011, was a somewhat dull day. Many Christchurch people were out at lunch, or had just returned to work when at 12.51pm the earth commenced violently shaking, and lives were changed forever.

Buildings collapsed, people died or were badly injured, and prized possessions fell off shelves and out of cupboards, smashing onto the floor below. In that moment both valuable possessions and lives were shattered. This was a moment in time—just another story in our lives. Tragic as this event may be, it marked the beginning of this book of short stories.

"Moments in Time", reminds us that every day is a unique experience and not always a bunch of roses. As you will find in this book there will be stories of good times, and times to laugh about. But there will also be earthquakes in our life. Similarly to the people of Christchurch we need to rise to these occasions and be resilient. There is always hope; light at the end of the tunnel, even though there may be a few trains in between.

Brian Wilson

MOMENTS IN TIME

At one time life was kind to me.
Was young and full of energy.
I could see and hear and run
Play sport and have a lot of fun.

But time is cruel it takes away
The things we would have rather stay.
What we take for granted slowly passes
Memory, sight; where are those glasses?

And what we have we do not own
Life's things we treasure, they're all on loan
We are simply actors playing different roles
In seasons, moments and with different goals.

The child of spring—a time of learning
Summer's young—with passion burning.
Then comes the fall; the autumn stage
And winter follows middle-age.

Time is a journey; a game of seasons,
Often there's no rhyme, nor reasons.
It's a collection of life's short stories
And beyond lies eternity with all its glories.

Brian Wilson

THE PSYCHOLOGIST

THE PSYCHOLOGIST RESTED against the wall of the Sydney (Australia) underground station. It was still early; the station platform was almost deserted. Apart from a tramp walking towards him, there was just a scattering of some school children at the far end. Soon, there would be a constant stream of traffic as workers arrived and boarded trains for home. This would be the prime time to observe people, one of his favourite pastimes. Meanwhile, he would have to resign himself to watching the lowly figure of the tramp.

This despicable figure was of average build, somewhat stooped, and aged somewhere in his late 70s. He fitted the stereotype of most tramps, being gaunt, unshaven and dishevelled. Like most tramps, his flushed complexion was most probably indicative of alcohol abuse, as opposed to a coronary problem. He certainly did not look a healthy sight. As the tramp drew closer, he looked vaguely familiar. This was not unexpected, as the psychologist had most probably seen him scavenging around before. The tramp sauntered over to a rubbish bin, carefully picking his way through its contents. One item he retained (and folded neatly) was a newspaper. The psychologist was somewhat perplexed. What would a tramp, a person living from day to day with no interest in the world, want with a newspaper? This was indeed unexpected behaviour. It tended to contradict the general perception of a tramp as being an uneducated no-hoper. But as a psychologist, he looked beyond stereotypes. Couldn't a tramp have also once been somebody successful and educated?

In contrast, the psychologist was well dressed. He ran a successful practice and could afford to purchase his clothes at places such as David Jones and Myers. Today he wore a smart pair of dark blue, pin striped trousers with an open-neck pale blue, silk shirt. Life had been good to him. He had completed his doctorate at twenty-six and had been fortunate to have Higgins as his supervisor. Professor Higgins had been extremely helpful in guiding him through the process of research and in preparing his thesis. His guidance had made a somewhat stressful process uncomplicated. Now 45 years of age, the psychologist felt complacent; albeit arrogant. He had a wife and family, and was more than satisfied materialistically. His world had never been better. He could afford to finish work whenever he liked. It was interesting standing around in busy areas observing others. Today he was in fine form, as he decided to go a step further and try an experiment.

Over the many observations he had made at the railway station, he had often wondered what a person would do if they dropped something valuable onto the railway tracks. If it was something cheap like a comb, or even sunglasses, then they might simply accept the loss. In preparation for his experiment, he had earlier dropped a small bundle of $50 notes near the tracks. On his income this was not a great loss; but to many others it was an amount worth retrieving and a fortune for somebody as destitute as a tramp.

The tramp had also at one time been successful. In his prime he had been a highly paid lecturer leading an affluent lifestyle. But this all changed when his son committed suicide at the age of seventeen. He saw himself as being responsible, and the guilt he and his wife shared culminated in the dissolution of their marriage. From there it was all down hill: depression, an inability to work and manage his life savings, and now heart problems. He was struggling to just support himself, let alone being able to afford the needed medication for his high blood pressure. Therefore the discovery of a bundle of $50 notes on the railway track was a pleasant surprise; some resolve to his problems.

If he was quick the money would be his. But very soon the station would start filling with people. If he didn't take it now then somebody else would. At the same time he knew that the next train was due within minutes. Pressure mounted as he grappled with the ambivalence of need versus danger. Finally, he decided to make a grab for the money. As he stepped forward to the edge of the platform, the distant rumble of an approaching train through the tunnel could be heard. At the same time a sharp pain crossed his chest. He fell forward in front of the oncoming train.

The psychologist observed the incident. As the train screeched to a halt, people appeared from nowhere to observe the unfolding scene. He felt sick, guilty, and responsible. It was a silly experiment and would have never been passed by any ethics committee. He did not stay to learn that the tramp had died from a heart attack. Instead, he left the station upset, wishing he had never carried out such a foolish experiment. It may have been just a tramp, but this was still a person—maybe who had once been somebody important. That face did look very familiar.

"Oh no, I've killed Higgins."

ROOF OF EUROPE ON A PLATE

"COME ON," SCREAMED Joe, somewhat anxious. "We'll miss the train if you don't hurry up."

Wilmer was not going to be told what to do. She refocused her camera on some distant chalets and took another photo, then made a point of taking time out to put her camera back into her bag before strolling towards Joe and the train. Shortly after they had boarded and settled into two vacant seats, the train gave several lurches forward then began to gather momentum.

It slowly grunted up the steep snow-covered valley from Grindelwald. Ahead lay a rocky snow-clad Mt Eiger 3970m high. Joe and Wilmer sat back and enjoyed viewing the scenery out of the small carriage's window occasionally taking a photo.

"That is very impressive," commented Joe looking towards some chalets.

"What is?" asked Wilmer.

"Amazing; every one of these chalets has a neatly piled stack of firewood. Guess it must get very cold at times. Living here and enjoying this spectacular scenery must come at a price. I would think that the mountainous weather here can be very unforgiving with a lot of house maintenance required as well."

Wilmer didn't comment. Joe had to have an opinion on everything. He was probably right, but she didn't want to fuel his ego and get him started. Wilmer's silence though didn't stop Joe. When he had something to say he said it regardless.

"You know," he added, "we have it too good in New Zealand. Some people are so lazy they're even into paying somebody else to wash their car."

"It's worse in the USA," commented an American woman across the aisle. "A lot of people can't even be bothered with cooking and instead dine out most of the time."

"That's terrible," commented Wilmer.

"And the young people," added Joe. "They expect everything on a plate. Their first house has to be like their parents. You know my parents when they moved into their first house had packing boxes for seats."

"That's quite enough Joe," instructed Wilmer. "Just relax, sit back and enjoy the scenery."

The train now took a steeper path riding up and over a steep outcrop of rock on the lower slopes of Mt Eiger, then veered to the right. It continued to climb then, as the ground levelled, it drew to a halt.

"It's a station," Joe observed.

"I think this place is called Scheidegg," commented Wilmer, having just checked a brochure resting on her knees. "It's where we change trains."

"Gosh! These Swiss people are really very clever," stated Joe. "Shops and cafés on mountains." Joe adjusted his sunglasses to avoid the glare from the snow, as he looked across at the buildings. Wilmer got out her camera and took a photo of the buildings.

"Our train is over there," pointed Wilmer, conveniently changing the subject.

"The one to takes us to the top?" clarified her husband.

Wilmer nodded, and they crossed the railway lines to the adjacent platform. On boarding the train carriage they found two vacant seats. Wilmer reached into her purse and pulled out her digital camera.

"You'd better have the window seat," offered Joe standing and allowing Wilmer to slide past.

Soon there were a couple of jolts and they were on their way. Slowly the train inched its way up the steep slope. They passed a small glacier on their left, then they rounded a rocky ridge that seemed to stretch all the way down from the summit.

The train slowly grunted up the steep slope from Scheidegg.

Suddenly everything became dark as they entered into a tunnel and started an even steeper and slower ascent. They were now moving up through the bowels of Mt Eiger. Wilmer plugged her ears with her fingers.

"Are you ok?" asked a concerned Joe.

"Just my ears; they are clicking," replied Wilma.

"This is unbelievable," stated Joe. "To think, that man has managed to tunnel up through the inside of a mountain; absolutely amazing."

Wilmer just nodded in response. Perhaps having blocked ears had its advantages.

The train drew to a stop. Everyone got up and filed out. They headed for one of two observation points. These were holes cut out in the side of the mountain ceiled with thick glass windows. Through these people could look out of the mountain, and follow the Eiger's snowy and rocky precipitous slope to the valley below.

After about 5 minutes everyone returned to the train, which now continued on its journey climbing even higher. Eventually it stopped again, and everyone disembarked to look out from a much higher observation point.

"It's hard to know which mountain we are in now," said Joe as the train continued to climb first through Mt Eiger, then Mt Monch, ending up near the top of Mt Jungfrau.

Finally the train came to rest at an underground station.

"Looks like we have reached the top of Mt Jungfrau," advised Wilmer.

"Where to now?" asked Joe.

"Let's just follow the crowd," suggested Wilmer.

They walked through a tunnel and entered a restaurant and viewing area. "Wow! What a view!" exclaimed Joe.

"It's certainly something to write home about," commented Wilmer.

They spent about fifteen minutes working their way through the cafeteria, souvenir shop and restaurant areas before taking the lift up to the snow caves. In the snow cave Joe marvelled at the ice carvings. Wilmer was quite content taking lots of photos of these. She could later show the photos to her grandchildren.

"Well time to go up to the Sphinx," declared Joe. The Sphinx is the highest observation point sitting at 3454m, or 11,333 feet. From this point one can look out upon the roof of Europe. Joe enjoyed this view and stood in awe at the spectacular scenery of mountains and valleys, while Wilmer snapped as many photos as she could.

"Really ingenious," declared Joe.

"What is?" asked Wilmer.

"This whole place; the train, everything. It was very expensive coming up here, but worth every penny. Because of Swiss ingenuity, we are now effortlessly standing 11,000 feet on the roof of Europe."

"It is very clever," agreed Wilmer.

His jaw suddenly dropped and his mood suddenly changed, as his eyes caught sight of the largest man and woman he had ever seen.

"But you know that's what is really wrong with the world. Nowadays everything is too easy."

"Where's he heading now?" thought Wilmer, who had some large, black mountain birds in her camera sights.

"Well, think of the mountaineer who has trained hard over months, or even years just to be fit enough to climb this mountain. Through sheer determination and perseverance; exhausted and drenched in sweat, he finally crawls onto the summit, only to find that fat unfit couple over there. How do you think he would feel?"

"How do you think he would feel if he saw you, a sixty-year old man, instead?" pointed out Wilmer. "Besides you can't call people fat. You just don't do that; it's rude."

"Fat is fat," replied Joe. "We can't say they are skinny, nor can we say they are normal size. They are FAT."

The next morning they were walking along the road to a restaurant in Grindelwald when Joe began to shrug. Wilmer saw a very large man walking towards them.

"What's wrong?" she enquired.

Joe shrugged his shoulders. "It's so, so cold, I should have brought my jacket," he replied. "Brrr"

"You wouldn't be cold if you put on a bit more weight," commented the very large man, who at this stage was walking past. "You know Switzerland is not a place for skinny people!

SPLIT ENDS

"GARY, I DESPAIR of you," declared Laura.

"Well, I don't care," Gary replied. "I've a bottle of wine in my suit case and I don't want this getting broken. The baggage handlers don't care. They throw these cases around you know. The best place is my hand luggage, but you're not allowed; they're paranoid about bombs. You just can't win." Gary continued to meticulously arrange his suitcase, while Laura looked on despairingly. Her case was already packed and she was ready to go.

"Come on," Laura demanded. She cast an anxious look at her watch and moved closer to the door, bag in hand. Gary was, however, either oblivious to her body language, or simply chose to ignore it.

"Gary, check-in at Coolangatta airport is in five minutes. Come on!" Her voice was now showing signs of stress.

Gary though seemed unperturbed, and continued to sort out his suitcase. Laura did tend to stress out and after all, check in time is not when the plane is leaving.

"Now what!" she snapped, as Gary started to rearrange his hand-luggage.

"I need to rearrange this too," he responded. "I have presents in here for the kids and need to use some of my clothes for padding."

"For goodness sake, we really need to go," bellowed Laura.

Gary continued placing clothing around the various presents while Laura became more and more agitated. She was now halfway out the hotel room door. Finally, to Laura's disbelief, Gary pushed the suitcase shut and declared: "Done."

"And not a minute before time," responded Laura sarcastically. "Now come on or we will miss our flight."

Unlike Laura, Gary was very particular about his suitcase being neat and tidy, and breakable items being well padded. This approach extended to his dress. While Laura was comfortable boarding the plane in a light, blue sun frock, Gary preferred to look more formal. In this case, in the absence of a suit, his navy, work trousers and matching shirt and tie would have to suffice. Exiting and entering countries, he believed, justified dressing in formal attire.

At the airport Laura was less stressed, and even somewhat more relieved once the suitcases had been checked through and well out of Gary's reach. For her the whole travel exercise of packing bags, baggage check-in, paper work and customs, was a stressful ending to an otherwise pleasant two weeks holiday.

"Let's have a coffee, it will be good for my nerves," she suggested. They looked around and found two high bar stools where they could sit and enjoy a coffee. The seats were very wide. Gary placed his Latté on the table and swung himself onto the bar stool.

"Oh no," cried Gary as he sat down, "I've split my pants."

"For goodness sake!" exclaimed Laura. "You have my nerves on edge all the time."

Gary nervously explored the damage zone. It was worse than he could have ever imagined. The split was extensive with most of the seam at the back having parted. He removed his jersey and tied it around his waist to cover his embarrassment, then carefully removed himself from the seat.

"Where are you going?" asked a now amused Laura, who had started to see the funny side as well as his back side.

"I'll be back shortly," replied Gary.

Soon after, Gary returned with a satisfied look. Laura looked at Gary, somewhat surprised at his composure.

"Well, I've been to the stationery shop and the men's toilets," he explained. "At the stationery shop I purchased a role of sticky tape, and in the toilet I repaired the split by taping over the seam." Gary, quite pleased with his Kiwi ingenuity in resolving the problem, returned to place himself on the bar stool.

"Uh," grunted Gary.

"What is it now?" asked Laura. "I think I am going to need a stronger cup of coffee," she added.

"It's pulled apart, AGAIN," replied Gary, now not so pleased with himself.

"Well you're just going to have to display your wares," Laura said with a giggle.

It was now time to concede defeat, and at best minimise the embarrassment. The jersey tied around his waist would suffice.

Going through Australian customs was quite unsettling for Gary. He insisted Laura walk close behind just in case he gaped. As Gary approached the metal detector he removed his belt.

"I'll need your jersey too as it has a zip," demanded the customs official.

"But, I've split my pants," whispered Gary.

"He said he split his pants," announced Laura in a much louder voice.

Several customs officials looked over in Gary's direction somewhat amused.

"Put your jersey in this tray," said the customs official.

Gary reluctantly removed his jersey and scampered through the metal detector, then quickly snatched up his jersey and returned it to his waist. At the exit door some custom officials were carrying out a hand metal detector check of an elderly couple.

"Hip replacement; probably," whispered Laura.

"Well, it's hardly likely to be for drugs," replied a rather red faced Gary.

"Do you need to check us?" offered Laura.

"What? No!" mumbled Gary, cringing then scowling at Laura.

What was Laura thinking of? She didn't need to volunteer.

"No, I think we have seen quite enough," quipped the customs officer with a smirk on her face looking towards an even more flushed Gary.

During the three hour flight his jersey remained firmly around his waist. In fact, it never left his waist until he was back home in Christchurch.

Once home, he quickly replaced his trousers then launched into the seemingly onerous task of unpacking his bags. Laura wisely retreated to the kitchen and made a cup of coffee. This would be good for her nerves. Besides, she didn't want to once again endure this painful experience.

"Laura," called out a somewhat embarrassed Gary.

"What!"

"I've just been getting the children's gifts out of my hand luggage. Yes nothing is broken, but do you know why?"

"Yes, I know. It's because you took painful hours organising your case."

"Sort of, but also because I had the gifts carefully wrapped up under my spare trousers!"

A DAY TO REMEMBER
PART ONE

"LANGUAGE SCHOOL, I think," commented Bruce, as he sipped his tea and peered out the window.

"What are you looking at?" enquired Alex.

"CTV building," replied Bruce.

"Oh! The Canterbury Television building. Yes, there are all sorts of people there. Doctors, dentists, counsellors—you name it," said Alex biting into his ham sandwich.

"So, where are all the TV bods then?" asked Bruce.

"Perhaps television companies only require a small number of staff, or they have a lot of field staff," suggested Alex.

"Guess you're right," replied Bruce.

"Think about it," added Alex. "TV crews are out and about all the time filming and gathering news."

"Guess so. Life must be so unpredictable for TV crews," commented Bruce. "They turn up to work, only to find they're running around town like headless chooks after a news breaking story. Who knows what the day will bring. There are no certainties in life,"

"Indeed, apart from death and taxes," stated Alex. They both laughed.

"My uncle always used to say that you never know what's around the corner," Bruce commented, as he started to peel a banana.

"Just watch what you're biting on then," said Alex jokingly. Alex ate the remaining ham sandwich in his lunch bag, then announced, "Just to change the subject, I'm off to do some shopping for a hacksaw blade."

"Shouldn't break the bank," said Bruce.

"No," replied Alex. "But do you know there are hacksaw blades in our civil defence equipment—goodness knows what for."

"You're not still involved with civil defence?" enquired Bruce somewhat surprised.

"Yes, the key-holder for the equipment cabinet," replied Alex.

"Don't know why you bother to stay on," commented Bruce. "I do my job, get paid and that's it. Why on earth do other stuff like civil defence? Tell you what, if there was a civil emergency, I for sure wouldn't be sticking around here. I'd be off home like a shot. Stuff rescuing others; family, friends and my own safety are much more important. There's no reward for heroes."

Alex shook his head. "Can't agree," he said.

"Anyhow, that's my lunch break," added Bruce screwing up the lunch wrapping paper into a neat ball and firing it in the direction of the rubbish bin. "It's back to work. I've got to get a letter done. It's due to go out on the 22nd of February."

"That's today," said Alex.

"Exactly, that's why I have got to make tracks," replied Bruce reluctantly rising from his comfortable seat. "If I don't do the work, then I don't get paid. Now that is what really matters."

Bruce returned to his desk, and Alex set out into town to get his hacksaw blade.

Alex was satisfied having purchased his hacksaw blade, and was walking down Cashel Street. It was 12.51pm. Suddenly, he heard a loud roaring noise. Before he could investigate, by looking around, the ground under his feet started shaking violently. He struggled to stay on his feet. At the same time it became difficult to breathe as the air was filled with white dust. Overhead, masonry started breaking and crashing down onto the street. He could see people on the street in a mad panic. They were running, as best they could, from the falling debris.

Alex took refuge under the wooden veranda of the Grumpy Mole tavern. He now had something to hold onto, and was able to stay on his feet. A screaming mother and her dazed son passing by looked hopelessly lost in the confusion not knowing which way to turn. Alex reached out and pulled them in under the safety of the veranda. Across the road the 26 storey Hotel Grand Chancellor had separated from the car park building and now looked to be on a lean. The street had started to buckle in places as the ground shaking continued. This was unbelievable. Alex, over the last five months, had experienced over three thousand earthquakes and aftershocks; but nothing close to being as violent, destructive and life threatening.

"My, gosh!" thought Alex, as the shaking gave no suggestion of stopping. "This is a massive earthquake."

It seemed to be far more powerful than the 7.1 Richter scale, earthquake that rocked Christchurch New Zealand, in September, and at 12.51 it was certainly not a good time for this to happen. It was lunch time and a working day. The central business area would be packed with people. There could be hundreds or thousands of people killed.

After the shaking had ceased he walked back to work. There would be a real need for those with civil defence training. He took the safer route down the middle of the road away from falling debris. The footpath was now no longer a safe place to walk. One building (still intact) had showered it with head size pieces of masonry. Another building had a large crack down the façade and posed as a potential threat when the aftershocks came. Further down the road, Alex stopped in horror. Ahead was an empty section.

"I'm sure there was a building here," he thought. "No, if there was a building here it wouldn't just collapse, even if the earthquake was large. But no, there was a building here. My, gosh! The CTV building has collapsed." Alex eyes scanned the site and focused on a pile of rubble. So this was it—the CTV building? Now only the top two floors could be identified. Where were all those people they had observed only twenty minutes ago?

He was stunned and found it difficult coming to terms with this pile of rubble being the CTV building. It just didn't make sense. How can a six story building simply collapse especially with modern building techniques? He was angry. Somebody had to be held accountable. Something wasn't done right in the construction, or design for it to collapse.

Alex returned to his workplace and negotiated his way through an exodus of traumatised staff evacuating the building. Some looked quite pale and distressed, while others were trying to reach friends and family on their cell phones. On reaching his office, he recovered his personal civil defence rescue gear then made his way back out of the building to the CTV site. The Police were already there. Workmen from the Samoan church across the road were also helping along with some passers-by and work colleagues. Fortunately, there were also two doctors on the site.

The group started moving debris off the pile foolishly believing they would find survivors. They were assisted by two heavy earth moving machines that had been working on the adjoining demolition site. The group removed two bodies and three seriously injured. A number of people in the top two storeys were able to escape, but there was little hope for those buried, especially when a fire started from under the rubble.

There was a lot of confusion and running about, no stretchers, and little in the way of rescue supplies. He had been trained in civil defence, but in training you have all the required equipment plus the team you have trained with.

"Rescue equipment, we need rescue equipment," bellowed a frustrated policeman.

"And some boots my size," added an optimistic policewoman in high heels, who was standing at the edge of the rubble feeling quite useless.

"Dream on, there's little chance of getting boots and your size," shouted another policeman. "We can be certain of that."

Alex approached the policeman.

"We have civil defence equipment in our building, but I will require help bringing this out."

Some policemen and a number of other helpers, accompanied Alex and together were able to remove all the civil defence supplies. The large bags contained bottles of water, ropes, stretchers, blankets, first-aid equipment, hacksaw blades and other useful items. As they unpacked the supplies, Alex suddenly turned around and shouted across to the police woman.

"You really won't believe this, but I have found you some work-boots, and they look to be about your size."

Alex was also surprised to find why hacksaw blades had been included. They were effective in cutting through the CTV iron roof.

He continued to help working his way through the rubble hoping to find somebody alive. But as the hours passed by, hope faded. Every now and again he would try ringing his wife to let her know he was safe. But it was to no avail; the cell phone network was down.

It was now 5.30pm and there seemed little chance of finding any further live bodies. "I hope you don't mind, but I think I will go home now," he told a policeman. "It would be good to see that my own family is safe."

"Thank you for all your help," replied the policeman, "most people would have gone straight home after the earthquake."

"So I found out from a mate at lunch time," commented Alex.

Alex reluctantly left behind the site and made his way home. He was later to learn that the shaking was a shallow 5km deep, 6.3 Richter scale, earthquake on an unknown fault-line near to the city. This ended up levelling much of the city taking 186 lives and destroying over half the buildings in the central business area. That day, 116 people died in the CTV building collapse. For many days rescuers worked at the CTV site recovering bodies.

February 22nd 2011
Earthquake damage to shops central city

February 22nd 2011
Check Mate (Cathedral Square following the earthquake)

A DAY TO REMEMBER
PART TWO

BRUCE MADE HIS way back down from the cafeteria. So that was lunch. He had a letter that needed to go out today; no matter what. If you want to move on up the promotion ladder, then you focus on the job delivering the required output. You don't get it from contributing to "no-thanks" activities like civil defence.

He was reflecting on the conversation he had with Alex, his work colleague, in the cafeteria. Bruce did not share Alex's enthusiasm for civil defence, especially when they occupied a safe modern building.

It was interesting though, their conversation about the CTV building. Who would think that in addition to the television company employees, there were floors occupied by doctors, counsellors, language schools and other groups? The place was obviously a hive of activity.

"Enough of this thought, I have a letter to get out." Bruce typed the 22 February 2011 at the top of his letter and added the address. He began to type the body of the letter. "Dear Sir, thank you for your letter of the . . . ."

Suddenly, the building started to shake. Bruce stopped typing and held on to the desk. Someone screamed. "Another one of these frustrating aftershocks," he muttered, somewhat blasé. Then looking towards the screen he contemptuously continued with the letter. Since September last year he had experienced many aftershocks. Some had been as large as 5 on the Richter scale. In comparison, this one was big.

The computer screen fell on to the desk. This had never happened before with an aftershock. Bruce put it back upright, and this time chose not to continue until the shaking stopped. "The shaking should stop soon," he thought. But the shaking continued and instead grew in intensity. This was not at all like the other aftershocks. It was more intense and violent. He looked around. While he continued to rock sideways in his chair his work colleagues had moved under their desks. Bruce decided to also take cover.

Finally, after about twenty seconds, the shaking ceased. All he could see through the windows was a cloud of white dust—somewhat whiter than the pale complexion of his work colleagues. He picked up his computer screen that had again fallen during the shaking. His computer hard drive had been thrown out of its mounting and had become unplugged. He had just set about plugging the connections back into his computer when the fire alarm sounded.

"Everyone out," shouted his boss.

Bruce continued to fix his computer. That letter must go out.

"Bruce! No time for that. We are all evacuating the building," instructed his boss.

Bruce reluctantly joined the exodus of pasty, frightened faces slowly descending the stairway. Some were trying to reach friends and family on their cell phones. But it was to no avail as the networks had crashed. The enormity of the situation was now starting to hit Bruce. This was not simply another aftershock. Who knows, there could be fatalities. Bruce was now deeply concerned as he evacuated the building.

"It's really awful, there have been people buried under falling debris in town," commented a distraught work colleague, standing on the pavement outside. Bruce froze for a second, and felt nauseous. This was indeed a bad situation.

He joined the procession of seemingly dazed work colleagues heading for the assembly point. Passing his boss he informed her, "I'm going home," then continued to remain with the group.

Seeing the pile of rubble from fallen buildings alerted Bruce to the likelihood of more death and destruction as large aftershocks would follow. He needed to get home. Had his wife and children survived? Were they well prepared for survival—if his house was still standing? There could be power and water cuts.

Bruce broke from the group, and set off for his car. He headed away from the central business area to avoid falling debris. Ahead of him a broken pipe under the road had burst and he had to wade through a flooded area of footpath. At another intersection a tradesman had taken the initiative of positioning himself in the middle of the intersection and was directing the traffic, as the traffic lights had ceased working. He passed scores of building now lying in ruins. Further up the road Bruce came across a small group of people deep in conversation about events across the road.

"The parking building has collapsed and we think people are trapped in there," one told Bruce. Fortunately Bruce had parked on the road and his car was undamaged. It was critical that he get home quickly to check up on family.

The roads were already congested with traffic, as people urgently headed home for similar reasons. Despite the urgency, like others, he had to tolerate the heavy traffic flow and dead traffic lights as he drove out of the central business area. Bruce however, skilfully avoided traffic jams by reinventing his route home wherever he could.

Surprisingly, he arrived home quite quickly given the heavy traffic. At first glance, the house looked pretty intact, apart from a couple of bricks having fallen from one side. In trepidation he slowly opened the door. What he found could only be described as a war zone. He was greeted by a sickening smell; a mixture of coffee, wine, chocolate drink and other ingredients spewed out from the pantry across the kitchen floor. Added to this unpalatable cocktail were pieces of broken cups, glasses, and bowls, thrown out from the cupboards above.

**Amongst this sickening mess was an unbroken cup
with a message. "In everything give thanks."**

After negotiating his way across the minefield of broken glass and
crockery, he reached the cold water tap and filled up containers with
what remaining water he could retrieve.

Frustration; his cell phone line was dead and the power was off. The
landline was also inoperable. He had no way of knowing if his family
were safe. It was a case of waiting to see which family members would
turn up.

Would his wife be safe, as she worked in a very old building? Apart
from the CTV building which had collapsed, it did seem to be the older
buildings that were now in ruins.

He set out to examine his house and property for further damage,
before starting to clear up the mess of broken kitchen-ware, antiques,
vases and electrical appliances. Bruce was ever hopeful, when searching
through the debris of finding some treasured possession still intact. The
place was a mess. They had lost so much.

A face appeared at the door. It was his son-in-law. "Thank goodness
somebody else is safe," Bruce said. "Justine?"

"Yes, your daughter is well and safe," reassured his son-in-law.

Shortly after, his son arrived home. "Have you heard from your mum?" Bruce asked.

"No," his son Mark replied. "But it is not good, Dad, her side of town," he added. "The radio said that the east side of town where she works got a hammering. A lot of the roads there are flooded due to liquefaction and burst pipes. There was also talk about some cars and cyclists being swallowed up by big holes suddenly opening up in the road. Sorry, Dad, it doesn't sound good."

It seemed that hours had ticked by, but his wife had still not arrived home. About an hour later the door opened and his wife appeared. She told stories of flooded roads, big bumps in the roads and very heavy traffic.

Who would have thought that this could happen in Christchurch— at one time considered the least likely city in New Zealand to have a large earthquake?

DOWN TIME

IT WAS THE 31st March, now just over one month since the 6.3 Richter scale earthquake flattened much of Christchurch, New Zealand. Still the aftershocks kept rocking the city daily. The people of Christchurch had endured more than enough, having experienced over 5000 aftershocks since the 7.1 earthquake on the 4th of September.

Many elderly people had been moved out of Christchurch due to the shaking or damage to their homes or rest-homes. Other people had used the opportunity to take a holiday away from Christchurch, while a smaller number had called it quits and relocated to another town or city.

Gavin had also had enough. His workplace, although structurally sound, was centred in the "red zone", an area in the central business district. This was closed to all but emergency groups. It was unlikely that he would be able to return to this building this year, as large buildings, like the 26 storey Hotel Grand Chancellor crippled by the 22nd February earthquake, would have to be demolished. He had been given a laptop, and was expected to work from home. His world had been turned upside down. He now no longer went to work so seldom saw his work colleagues. Half the time he couldn't even remember what day it was, as his whole life was in disarray.

At home things were no better. The house was a write-off, though safe to live in. Some doors would not close and some windows wouldn't open. After every big aftershock the hot water cylinder began to leak again. Then there was the added hassle of having to be available for various tradesmen, damage assessors and loss adjusters. Capping all of these frustrations, was the uncertainty surrounding future city land use, and the insurance companies' hesitation to commence repairing or replace dwellings until the politicians had come to a decision and the shaking ceased. Meanwhile, one was left to persevere with living in a broken home and watching the cracks grow bigger with each large aftershock.

It was also disappointing for Gavin to go to a restaurant and find it had been demolished, or to his favourite electronics shop and find it closed due to earthquake damage. Gavin was not a happy man. He felt frazzled and flat, and at times was quite grumpy.

"That is it," Gavin said closing his laptop. "I'm finished for the day. Nothing's gone well today. The computer link keeps crashing and twice I lost all my work."

"Well, you don't need to worry about it any more today," reassured Susan.

"My, I am certainly looking forward to the weekend and the breakfast with the baby boomers," Gavin sighed.

"Yes, you certainly like your breakfasts," stated Susan. "But as for me, I'm not really a breakfast person."

Every month the "baby boomers", a group of friends went out for breakfast. This Saturday, was set for a buffet breakfast—Gavin's favourite.

Gavin retreated to the lounge and flicked on the television. It wasn't as if he had anything he wanted to watch. Most of the stuff he thought was rubbish anyway. He just wanted to blob out on the couch. With the earthquake he had become more lethargic during the day, and was sleeping too long at night. Despite all his hang-ups, that night he again slept very well.

The next morning, rather uncharacteristically, he was up and dressed by 8am. Susan, though, was still in bed.

"You're going to need to get up soon," Gavin reminded Susan.

"No I don't. It's my day off," replied a half-asleep Susan.

"But we have to leave for the breakfast . . . it's at eight-thirty."

"Don't be silly, just let me sleep," said Susan rolling over to face the other direction. She was not at all interested in getting up.

"Women," Gavin muttered. Obviously, she has decided not to go. "Well, I'm going whether she comes or not."

Gavin got into his car and drove to the breakfast place arriving there at about 8.30am. He scanned the area to see where the baby boomers were sitting.

"Must be the first to arrive," he thought.

After half an hour of waiting he returned home. Susan was now up.

"Well, I guess you at least tried to fool me," said Susan.

"What do you mean?" asked Gavin. "I went to the breakfast place, but nobody turned up. It was this Saturday wasn't it?"

"Yes, but today is Friday, and April fools day," replied Susan.

Christchurch Cathedral in ruins after the February earthquake

EARTHQUAKES

Earthquakes, aftershocks, go we pray
Mother Earth's now had her way.
Destroyed our heritage, our city,
A real mess, oh what a pity!

The ground it's shaken, rocked and rumbled
Our buildings in response they crumbled.
Buried bodies—death, destruction,
Shattered lives—shock, dysfunction.

Rolling, bowling, the ground it's shifting,
Shaking, breaking, dropping, lifting.
Homes destroyed, land reduction,
Buckled roads and liquefaction.

Nothing left now all is gone,
Just hope we have to carry on.
To see the end of all this shaking,
Especially with a new year breaking.

Brian Wilson

A MOMENT OF TRUTH

"EXCUSE ME SIR, this is embarrassing, but can you tell me where I am? I need to find my way out of this place and get home. My wife and family will be wondering where I am."

The elderly mans kind eyes looked at Derek and he gently replied, "Your family already knows where you are, there is no need to worry. To find your way you will need to follow your heart."

Derek looked somewhat perplexed. "What a weird response."

Before Derek could enquire further the elderly gentleman had disappeared amongst the crowd of people. The place was packed, and noisy. There seemed more and more people coming all the time. Outside there were roads leading in all directions and it was difficult to know which road to take without a map and sign posting. "Follow your heart," what a weird thing to say.

"Excuse me madam, can you tell me where I might find a public phone?" enquired Derek.

The lady laughed. "Not in this place dear?" she replied, before she also disappeared.

Derek, observed the people coming and going. Many also looked lost and were asking around. At one stage Derek thought he saw an elderly lady—Mrs Lantree, who went to his church. But he was obviously mistaken, as she had been institutionalised due to having Alzheimer's. That's it. Could he be in some institution? Had he gone mad?

"Hello!" Now that was a familiar voice. It was Jenny, Derek's wife.

"Oh! Thank goodness, I thought for a moment that I was in a nut house. Was I supposed to meet you here, or have you come to pick me up?" asked Derek.

"Neither dear," replied Jenny. "Do you not know where you are?"

"I haven't the foggiest," stated Derek. "Don't tell me I had a stroke, or accident and I am in a nut house. Have I lost my marbles?"

"You don't recall three days ago driving over the Port Hills to pick up your son from camp and you went off the road?" asked Jenny.

"So that's it," responded Derek. "I had an accident and now have a brain injury."

"No dear, much worse."

"What happened? What happened? I'm not . . . ."

"Yes dear, you went off the road and dropped seventy metres," informed Jenny.

"Then how come you're here?" asked Derek. "This doesn't make sense."

"Two days after your accident, I was in town when a massive earthquake hit the city. I was hit by falling debris," explained Jenny.

"How terrible," Derek replied. "Then who is looking after the boys?"

"I wondered about that too," shared Jenny.

"Where do we go now? An elderly man said to follow my heart."

"Good advice," commented Jenny. "We don't want to end up in the other place, do we now?"

"No! My gosh, no," replied Derek. "I hadn't thought of that. But I really don't think I can make the journey now . . . I feel too tired."

"What's that?" enquired Jenny.

"I'm too tired," mumbled Derek.

"But you will need to get up soon," replied Jenny. "You have got a long drive over the Port Hills. You can't have your son standing around waiting to be picked up."

"Sorry! What? I must have been dreaming."

"What were you dreaming about dear?" asked Jenny.

"You know, I can't really remember. Yes you're right, I better get up otherwise James will be left waiting for me."

A FINE FAREWELL

"WELL, WE ARE here honey," announced Steve.

"This is Collingwood?" enquired Sally.

"Yes, I know it's small, but it's quite remote, beautiful and romantic," explained Steve. "One of the hidden treasures of New Zealand," he added.

They drove into the camping ground, and were met by a youngish man in his 30s who introduced himself as the owner.

"Gidday, ya have a cabin booked?" he asked.

"Mr and Mrs Smith," said Sally.

"Cool, the honeymooners," commented the owner.

"Doing a spot of sightseeing ah!" he added.

"Um, Farewell Spit. We were thinking of going there tomorrow," said Steve.

"Sweet," replied the owner.

"Ah, how far is it from here?" asked Steve.

"About 20km from Collingwood. Are ya booked on a tour?" enquired the owner. "Van leaves here eight sharp."

"No, we thought we would do our own thing and may be walk to the end," said Steve.

"Right," said the owner laughing, "I love ya dry sense of humour. Ya not a coaster by any chance?"

"No, I was being serious," commented Steve.

"Sure, go on and pull the other leg. Ah, the Spit stretches 26km. I think a bit far for ya to walk there and back in a day. Besides, there's quicksand in parts."

"What Steve meant was we will be going just a little way for a look," clarified Sally.

"Cool, now that's a different ball game," said the owner.

The next day, Sally and Steve were preparing breakfast in the communal kitchen, when a young woman in her mid-twenties approached them.

"I am Ingrid from Germany. I can join you today to Farewell Spit?"

"Of course you can," said Sally. "We will be leaving at 9.00am." Ingrid then went off to let her friends know, and Sally and Steve had breakfast.

"You're sure about Ingrid joining us Honey?" asked Steve. "After all, this is our honeymoon."

"It will be fine," replied Sally. "You have a whole lifetime of me ahead; enjoy the break. Do you think we will need to get a brochure or something as a guide?" asked Sally. "You know, we haven't been to Farewell Spit before."

"No need," replied Steve. "We have a road map. The Spit—well we can't really go wrong; she'll be right."

Shortly after, Ingrid reappeared dressed in jeans with an orange muslin dress on top, and the three set off to explore Farewell Spit.

"Park here," directed Sally, pointing to a grassy area at the start of Farewell Spit.

They parked the car and set off along a narrow strip of golden sand stretching into the horizon and bordered by sea and brush wood. It was a pleasant romantic walk along the narrow beach on a bright sunny day. Out at sea they could see an assortment of birds enjoying the serene conditions; diving, fishing and swimming amongst the calm waters.

By late afternoon the brush wood had disappeared and the narrow beach opened out into a fairyland of large golden sand dunes that rolled out into the horizon. Ingrid, somewhat enchanted, ran ahead taking photos of the dunes against a splendid sunset.

"What fantastic scenery, under a magnificent sunset," Steve declared.

"Sunset! Sunset!" repeated Sally. The spell was suddenly broken by a rude awakening. "If we don't hurry back, then we won't be able to see our way."

"Leave your photos Ingrid, we've got to get off the Spit before it gets dark," shouted Steve. "Hurry, hurry," he added.

Ingrid reluctantly abandoned her attempts to capture more of this magical moment, and rejoined the others. They started running back, but this time on the other side of the Spit. The beach here was a wide stretch of golden sand. It quickly became apparent that darkness was closing in very fast and they would not cover the required distance in daylight.

"I hate to say it, but we are going to have to spend the night on this Spit," declared Steve.

Sally looked at Ingrid "I know this isn't the best, but we can't wander down the beach in the dark. There is quicksand on the Spit," she said.

Steve guided them up to a grassy ridge well away from the reaches of the sea. Ingrid's dress shredded as they ploughed their way through the prickly brush. At the top they found a clear area to lie down and spend the night. Sally made sure she was positioned between Steve and Ingrid. The night was long and very cold, and all three desperately awaited the coming of dawn. With light breaking, they set off down the beach to their parked car.

Back at the camp, the owner was surprised to see them.

"Thought ya was motoring to Hanmer today," he said.

"Ah, yes that's right we are," replied Steve suddenly remembering they needed to have left early for the long drive. "We ended up spending the night on Farewell Spit."

"Sure! Ya trying to take the micky out of me again?" the owner replied.

"No, it is true," reassured Sally.

"Ya must be keen then. Few months earlier ya would have been eaten alive by mosquitoes, and a few months later become ice-blocks," the owner stated.

"Take it ya had a good time?" he asked sarcastically turning to Sally.

"No, it was horrible, I froze all night," replied Sally, "and during the long cold night there seemed to be all sorts of creepy crawlies."

"I can't agree," answered Steve. "It wasn't all that bad—at least for me. After all, how many guys get to spend a honeymoon night with two women?"

ON THE MOVE AGAIN

"THIS WILL BE good for you dear, helping your son move. It's good father-son bonding."

"But, I'm 59 years old and not as strong as I used to be," replied Graham.

"I'm sure it will be a breeze; just a bed, study desk and a few smaller items. Probably an hour's hard work at most," reassured Christie. "Really, he's just a student without a bean to his name; he won't have much."

"We will see," mumbled Graham somewhat apprehensive.

"Besides, you will enjoy the break. It will be like a holiday," added Christie.

"Sure," murmured Graham.

Graham reluctantly picked up his sleeping bag and an overnight bag and stretcher, and put them in the car.

"Won't need that dad," advised Isaac, his 21 year old son.

"Well! I'm past sleeping on a floor," snapped Graham.

"Won't need to, I have a spare mattress," replied Isaac.

It wasn't long before they were able to set off for Dunedin, a four to five hour's drive from Christchurch. Once having arrived at Dunedin it was hard finding a place to buy food as it was New Years Eve. There were only a few places open. In the end they settled for a pie from a corner dairy. After eating, Isaac drove Graham to his flat.

"Here's the guts of it," explained Isaac. "In Dunedin most students move flats on New Years Day."

"So when we move everything from here tomorrow, other people will be moving in at the same time?" replied Graham.

"Correct, and we can only move our stuff into the new flat after they have completed the inspection," added Isaac.

"Inspection?"

"The landlords, for the outgoing tenants," explained Isaac.

"And when does that take place?"

"Morning, sometime," replied Isaac.

"Oh! Well, I guess it still wouldn't hurt to start packing stuff in cartons now. Save time tomorrow," suggested Graham. "It sounds like its going to be chaos already."

The two methodically started packing away university text books and personal items. Soon they had created a wall of cartons. Graham looked at what was in the room and concluded that there were probably two trailer loads—a lot more than what Christie had suggested. But two trailers would be manageable.

"Hi Isaac."

Two young ladies appeared in the doorway.

"This is my dad," said Isaac.

"I'm Jenny, one of Isaac's flat mates, and this is a friend Sarah, who is staying tonight," said one of the girls.

"Are you going to hang out with us tonight?" Jenny asked Isaac.

"I can't," replied Isaac reluctantly. "I have Dad with me."

"He can come to," said Jenny. "We are just going over to the Octagon for the New Years Eve party."

"Well, you go Isaac," said Graham. "I'm quite happy staying here and watching telly."

"No we would like you to come too," insisted Jenny. "We won't be late as I have to get the bus to Christchurch at 7am tomorrow."

Graham agreed to join them, and later the four headed off to the free concert in the Octagon. The Octagon is the eight sided town centre of Dunedin, New Zealand's fifth largest city. After seeing the New Year in, they returned to the flat.

"Great concert," declared Isaac.

"Not really," replied Graham. "The music was far too loud and I didn't like the songs. They lacked the melodies of the 70s and 80s."

Isaac and Graham settled down for a good nights sleep in preparation for a busy New Years Day.

It was 8am when Graham awoke. He showered and dressed, then walked through the dining room to the kitchen. It was a typical student's flat. The musty smell, the dirty dishes stacked up waiting for a miracle, and the rubbish bags bursting at the seams waiting for the next collection day if someone remembered.

He boiled the jug and made a cup of tea in one of the tea stained cups, then took it into the dining room and sat down on a sofa. It was an old sofa and his bottom sunk deep down where there were once springs. The room was a mess with not only the sofa Graham was sitting on, but the back of another one in front, plus another two balanced on each other, plus several old television sets and other stuff. Isaac had explained that the flat was full of both incoming tenants' and outgoing tenants' furniture. This shambolic disarray of rubbish-dump type furniture was an ugly sight.

"Utter chaos," thought Graham as he cautiously slurped his hot tea.

A head suddenly popped up from behind the sofa in front.

"Oh! Sorry, I didn't know you were there," said an embarrassed Graham.

It was Sarah. She had been asleep on the sofa in front.

"That's OK, I'm a quiet sleeper," replied Sarah. "Jenny had to leave early and wanted to lock her room, so I crashed here for the night."

"Look, I'll give you privacy and drink my tea somewhere else," said Graham getting up and retreating towards the dining room door with a somewhat flushed complexion.

Graham finished his tea and finding Isaac still asleep, started to load the car up with the cartons. Eventually Isaac arose, quite unperturbed, and casually set about showering and having breakfast. Finally, Isaac was ready to leave and hire a trailer.

"Who are you calling?" Graham asked, as Isaac was keying his cell phone.

"I wanted to see if the girls wanted to go halves in the trailer, as I promised to move their stuff too," replied Isaac.

"You what! Isaac, I came to help you, I didn't come here to help all your friends as well," stated Graham. They collected the trailer and drove back to the flat. "Now, probably best to put the biggest stuff on first, like this bed," suggested Graham.

"I've also got some stuff in the dining room," said Isaac.

"What stuff?" enquired an anxious Graham.

"I have three suites."

"Three suites. What do you want three suites for?" asked a despairing Graham.

"To entertain of course."

"But don't your other flat mates have a suite?"

"Yes, of course."

They drove the first loaded trailer around to the flat. It was a commercial building converted into apartments.

"So what floor are you on?" enquired Graham nervously.

"I am on the third floor, so there are only three flights of stairs," replied Isaac.

"And of course a lift," added a presumptuous Graham.

"No, no lift. We have to carry everything up the stairs."

"The suites as well?"

"Yes, the suites too," replied Isaac.

They continued to load and unpack trailers, and carry furniture up stairways all day.

At 8pm Graham's cell phone rang.

"Hello."

"Hello dear," replied Christie.

"Hope you took your son out for a nice meal?"

"Christie dear, the last time I had something to eat was a pie at lunch time."

"Well, Graham it doesn't take that long to move a desk, bed and a few other things from one flat to another."

"Yes it does Christie, when it involves five heaped trailer loads and three flights of steps, not to mention three suites."

A SHAKY START

"YOU KNOW, I just have a feeling this trip isn't going to happen," said Karen as she got into the car.

"Well, I certainly hope your premonition is wrong. Getting up at 3am in the morning is definitely not me," replied Brian, "and this trip to the UK and Europe is one we have been planning for years."

Over the last two to three months, Brian had meticulously surfed the internet finding the best priced tours, and bed and breakfast accommodation for the areas they planned to visit. Any suggestions of things not working to plan did not bode well. He felt quite accomplished having saved thousands of dollars off what they might have paid travelling through Europe. Now he was looking forward to reaping the rewards—four-star accommodation at basement prices, a sixteen day coach tour through Europe, and the opportunity to visit relatives.

It was not only ridiculously early, but the morning was dark and cold. The streets were deserted, as they drove to the airport as most people were sensibly and snugly tucked away in bed; a place where Brian would rather be. Conversely, the airport at 4.30am was a hive of activity, as travellers arrived and departed, and those organised like Brian arrived early to secure a place near the front of the queues.

Brian and Karen near the front of the queue were satisfied knowing that they would be attended to in about 10 minutes. Soon their bags and tickets would be sorted out well before time, and they would be able to sit down, relax and await their flight. It was good to be organised.

Karen's premonition was simply unnecessary worry, as nothing could go wrong, when everything was so well planned.

At 4.34am, Brian, Karen and others while waiting in the queue were somewhat bewildered by an eerie noise that increasingly became louder.

"What is it?" Brian enquired.

Karen shook her head, while a girl standing nearby looked somewhat perplexed.

"Sounds like a plane, but you don't normally hear planes from this end of the airport," added Brian.

The noise continued, then suddenly stopped and the whole building started to shake violently. The Japanese people who had been in the queue were quick to position themselves against a wall and in a crouching position. Those left in the queue moved to stand against the other wall, as the walls and ceiling battled for position, and the floor rolled under foot. The ceiling tiles overhead threatened to fall, while chunks of plaster parted from the wall in places. Some people struggled to stay on their feet and were thrown down on the floor. Nearby, a large brochure stand was upturned and tossed across the floor, scattering brochures everywhere. Above all the noise glass could be heard breaking in other areas of the airport.

"Get over here Brian," Karen ordered. Brian had not moved from the spot he had earned in the queue. He reluctantly surrendered this position and joined the others by the wall. The shaking continued for a whole 40 seconds before it ended as suddenly as it had begun.

"Wow! That was one big earthquake," exclaimed Brian quickly returning to their place in the queue.

Suddenly, an alarm sounded and an announcement came to evacuate the airport building and assemble in the car park area. Everybody began evacuating the building to the car park area. Brian made sure they were in a good position to return quickly to the checkout. "Why should those who came late jump ahead?" thought Brian. "I had to sacrifice my warm cosy bed."

Outside in the car park hundreds of people assembled as the airport terminal emptied. Finally, the police secured the airport entrance ways and only police and trades-people entered the building. Taxis bringing new travellers continued arriving boosting the numbers of travellers waiting in the car park.

"Some people have just come from town, and said some buildings have collapsed and town is a mess," informed Karen.

"They didn't say how big the earthquake was?" Brian asked.

"7.1," said a stranger standing nearby, who was intently listening to a transistor radio. The stranger suddenly grabbed hold of a barrier bar as a large aftershock hit. Brian and Karen also tried to stay upright as the ground shook under their feet. The shake only lasted 5 or 6 seconds.

"That was another good shake," commented Brian.

"Nothing good about it," responded Karen.

"7.1, wow! I knew it had to be big," Brian exclaimed.

They continued to experience an uncomfortable wait in the cold of a dark morning. Finally, the all clear was given and the frozen travellers were invited to return to the warmth of the building.

"Quick!" Brian instructed. "We need to get back fast to regain our position in the queue."

Brian and Karen moved quickly through the entrance negotiating their way past other similarly anxious travellers intent on pursuing their plans. Finally they arrived at their counter securing a good position in the queue.

"Sorry folks," said the woman at the checkout counter. "There will be no planes arriving or leaving today. Our computers are out and at this stage we don't even know how safe the tarmac is."

Shortly after, an announcement came over the intercom.

"Please leave the terminal, all flights are cancelled today."

Karen looked over at Brian somewhat sympathetic as well as being disappointed. He had worked so hard planning the trip only for this to happen. She put her arm around his shoulders and gave him a hug.

"You know Honey," she whispered. "Your father often quoted Robbie Burns on the plans of mice and man."

BUFFET STOP-OVER

DEREK FELT UNCOMFORTABLE and pushed the attendants' button. An air hostess was soon standing next to his seat.

"You rang sir?" she asked.

"Yes, I have this terrible sinusitis and I was just wondering if you have anything I can take?"

"I will see what we have got sir."

It had been a long flight from London, so Derek was looking forward to getting some sleep that night during his two night stopover in Bangkok.

"Bangkok again," some of his work colleagues had said teasing him, when they found out he was stopping there. "People go there for one of two reasons: sex or drugs. Which is your reason?"

Derek knew that they were only joking, as he was known as a person of good moral standing. Besides, one would have to be extremely naïve to seriously believe this was why most people stopped at Bangkok. Thailand had far more to offer; the cheap hotels, markets, scenery, culture, beaches and of course the very cheap clothes and electronics. There were also some great day and half day tours.

"Here are some tablets, sir."

Derek took a tablet and tried to get some rest. It was only an hour to go until the plane landed at Bangkok. He loved Bangkok, especially for its cheap shopping. His mouth watered at the thought of buffet breakfast tomorrow morning at the Indra Regent Hotel. He couldn't make up his mind which he preferred most. Was it the two buffet breakfasts, where he could really pig-out, or the really cheap shopping? Tomorrow it would be all good: buffet breakfast, shopping and a chance to explore more of Bangkok.

The hour went quickly and it didn't seem that long after, that Derek found himself in a taxi heading towards the Indra Regent Hotel. After he arrived Derek threw down his bags and collapsed onto the bed. It was 5pm so he decided to have a nap before tea as he still felt unwell. In the past he had found sleep to be the most effective remedy for sinusitis. He lay on top of the bed not even bothering to take off his shoes, and closed his eyes.

He awoke sometime later and felt he had overcome his tiredness and sinusitis. It was now time to search out a tasty Thai evening meal. He was very hungry and loved Thai food: the spices, various rices and sauces. Then tomorrow, yum! Buffet breakfast. He would be able to help himself to generous servings of bacon and eggs, sausages, fried tomatoes, tropical fruit, various cereals; washed down with guava, mango, and other fruit juices. "I just love buffet breakfasts," he thought. Derek looked across at the bedside clock to adjust his watch to Thai time. "That can't be right. I arrived here at 5pm, had a nap, and now it is 10am!" He checked. The clock was definitely plugged into the wall and was on. But it could not be right. "I only had a nap so it should now be late afternoon and starting to get dark outside." Derek looked out the window. It was as bright as day. Below he could see part of the Pratunam Market set up along the pavement. The road was bustling with activity. "It's true; it must be the next day. Can I have slept for 17 hours? How can that be?" Derek quickly made his way down stairs to the hotel dining room lest he miss that buffet breakfast.

"Sorry sir, breakfast is over," he was told.

A disappointed Derek found the food barn within the adjoining shopping centre and settled down for a poor second, some rice and chicken.

After he completed his meal he made his way outside to the street market. It was a hot muggy 35 degrees outside the air conditioned shopping centre. The pavement was smothered by Asians and a thin scattering of European tourists. Derek kept his hand in his pocket, while he squeezed past shoppers, lest his wallet disappear. On one side of the pavement were shops and on the road side were street vendors. There were all sorts of things for sale such as clothes, jewellery, watches, cases, shoes and many other items.

"Rolex; very cheap; you buy; only 250 baht," came a voice from one of the street stalls.

"It's only a copy and too much," replied Derek.

"How much you pay?" asked the vendor.

"100 baht," said Derek.

"No, no, too cheap; you buy two watch then?" Derek shook his head and started to walk off.

"150 baht" yelled the vendor. "Very cheap," he added.

"120 baht," replied Derek.

"OK, OK," agreed the vendor. "Something for your lady too?"

"No," replied Derek handing over 120 baht.

Derek made his way into the covered part of the market where he found a woman vendor. He had dealt with her on previous trips. Derek gave her a list of the various clothes items he wanted to purchase and asked her for her best price. She got out her calculator and they agreed on the total price.

"Now for electronics," Derek thought, as he continued down the road squeezing his way past shoppers. The street market continued down another road to the right and he followed this to a pedestrian over bridge and the big computer and electronics centre. Inside were floors and floors of shops where you could buy software and a comprehensive range of electronic equipment. He was in his glory and spent the remainder of the day completing his shopping list.

Derek returned to the hotel satisfied that while he had missed his buffet breakfast, he had bought everything he had planned on buying.

The following morning he made sure to be on time for his buffet breakfast. Now fully fed and satisfied he was ready to return on the second leg of his journey to New Zealand.

WEET-BIX MOUNTAIN

"COME ON JOHN," shouted Andrew from about 20 metres away. I was so mesmerised by the scenery, that I hadn't realised the other two had started towards the river. I hoisted the heavy pack onto my back and trudged through the river gravel towards them.

It was like stepping out into a new world. Gone were the noises and smells of a concrete city. In their place was the tranquillity and freshness of the scenic Southern Alps of New Zealand. A place where man can join hands with nature; the winding mountain rivers threading their way through the white snow-capped mountains, the green native forests stretching down into the valleys to the rivers below, and the native bird life relishing the absence of a human-dominated environment.

We had arrived for our weekend break, and were now tramping up the Waimakariri River bed towards the mountains. Carrington—White hut was three hours steady tramping up the river. It is positioned at the junction of the White and Waimakariri Rivers. We hoped to reach this hut by dusk.

As expected, after several days of heavy rain, the river was up, but considerably more than anticipated. The first river crossing—usually a formality, this time required some respect, though posed no danger for three experienced trampers. In traditional river crossing style, we each waded diagonally across moving downstream with the current until we reached the other side. Having easily overcome the first obstacle, we continued towards a more formidable crossing—the second river braid.

In the past this crossing had also been relatively straightforward without the need for team work.

Andrew was first to reach the braid and found the widest and shallowest place to cross. It did not look at all like an easy crossing and it was apparent that for this crossing we would need to link arms. However Andrew, being Andrew, launched himself audaciously into the river before conceding that this one would require a team effort. We linked arms and stepped into the surging water exposing our legs to the tugging of the current, while the shingle under our boots rattled threatening to undermine our foothold. As we advanced the river grew deeper and the current more persuasive. We hadn't reached halfway before the water was licking our shorts.

"We need to turn back," I suggested.

"Just keep going," ordered a tenacious Andrew on our left.

"M . . . make up your minds," screamed Bruce, in the middle.

Suddenly, Bruce lost his footing and was at the mercy of the current. He frantically grasped my bush shirt sleeve with one hand, and Andrew's arm for dear life with the other. Together we were able to stabilise Bruce so he could regain a footing. Once all had recovered from this precarious situation, we sensibly withdrew to the river bank.

"Th . . . the rivers t . . . too dangerous to cross," stammered Bruce. "Besides, e . . . even if we made it to to the other side, th . . . the next crossing is even bigger." As a result we spent the night pitched in a tent beside the river.

In the mountains rivers rise and fall quickly. It was no surprise then to find that the river had receded the next day. Morning comes early in the mountains. First, one is overcome by the deafening chatter of birds. Then if this fails to arouse you, your sleep-in will surely be cut short as the sand flies invade the privacy of your tent and find a part of your face to stake a claim. It was not surprising then that we got started bright and early, and by 10am we had reached the Carrington-White Hut.

From the hut it is a three to four hour tramp up the White River to reach Barkers Hut, which is perched on a rocky outcrop below Mt Murchison. First there is a beautiful walk through a native beech forest frequented by tiny robins. This is followed by a walk alongside the White River to the top of the valley and foot of Mt Murchison.

At the top of the valley we came across a swing bridge stretched over a deep chasm. While it was not long, I hesitated at first conscious of the thirty pound pack on my back. A sudden jerk and this could throw me off balance, and send me plunging down to the chasm floor and almost certain death. Bruce and Andrew had been unperturbed about this crossing, and the narrow rock ledge which followed. They had confidently crossed over and disappeared around a rock on the other side. After nervously crossing over the chasm and edging my way along the ledge, I too rounded the rock. Andrew and Bruce were now some distance up a steep rocky slope on top of which the hut was perched.

The hut was the ideal place for a brew of tea and lunch. Bruce had the billy boiling by the time I had reached them. After lunch we were ready to move on. First, we stripped ourselves of our heavy packs leaving these in the hut. In their place we carried light day packs.

A kea (a green native mountain parrot) squawked as it soared overhead. On our right Murchison, the 2,408 metre high mountain, glistened in splendour, and was a magnet to our eyes. The White glacier flowing from just below the summit to the valley far below, would be our pathway. Soon at a higher level up the mountain we would be stepping foot on this glacier.

"Are y . . . you ready to go John?" Bruce asked.

"Yes, I replied."

Andrew was already making tracks up the gentle snow covered slope. The ridge eventually came to a point where we could step onto the glacier. Andrew was the first to test the ice, but had not stopped to put on crampons. He was quite happily zigzagging his way up the glacier with an ice axe in hand.

Bruce preferred my company. He realised the danger of crevasses and the safety of working together as we chose our steps up the glacier.

"N . . . no need for crampons," said Bruce. "The snow is is d . . . deep enough to to give a footing, but n . . . not t . . . too deep t . . . to hide small crevasses."

It wasn't long before Bruce and I had reached the foot of the summit. Bruce and I stopped and watched as Andrew clawed his way up the steep mud and rock slope to get to the summit ridge. As he climbed, he dislodged loose rocks.

"L . . . look out," cried Bruce, as a barrage of airborne rocks flew past.

Now it was Bruce's turn. This time more care was taken to avoid dislodging rocks. Bruce ascended the slope and scrambled out of sight. Now it was my turn. It was not easy making progress up the slope. My hand grips were suspect as the rock crumbled away in my hands. It reminded me of the breakfast cereal Weet-bix. It was a case of having to battle my way up the slope as my hand and feet grips kept sliding away. Finally, I too reached the summit and walked along the ridge to the highest point.

Bruce and Andrew had already been rewarded for their effort. Perched on the rocky peak they were enjoying a breathtaking view of a myriad of snow capped peaks. Below they could see blue mountain rivers meandering through green forest clad valleys. It was certainly a wonderful feeling being on the highest peak in the Arthurs Pass area and having such a panoramic view.

MUM

REST HOMES ARE not the most exciting places to go to. They remind me of libraries as they are so quiet you could hear a pin drop. Usually if you want to find one of the residents you look in one of three places: the entertainment areas—usually the television room, the dining area, or if still not successful then their bedroom.

The television room is the most popular room; this being somewhat ironic given that most residents have their own television set. It could be argued that they go there to socialise, but the room is usually dead quiet with those present mostly dozing, reading or knitting. Seldom do you see a resident engaging in conversation with another resident.

Today was no different to any other day. I entered the rest home, first sterilizing my hands from the bottle provided at the entrance. The place again was like a ghost town. It was so quiet; there wasn't a resident in sight. I tiptoed down the corridor to the TV room. Here I found the missing residents. Three rows of residents were seated facing the large television screen, though few were watching television. I scanned the area and concluded that Mum was not there. She was also not in the dining area as this was in between meal times. The dining tables were already set for the next meal but the area was unoccupied. I set off down another corridor and headed for her bedroom.

Ahead was a little old lady walking in the same direction. She was short, very grey, and stooped over a walking frame. Her steps were short and slow like she was walking on ice for the first time. She had purpose in her direction and persistence in achieving her goal, though it looked to be an effort to keep her heavily arthritic legs moving. I quickly caught up to her and hesitated to pass as she was unsteady on her feet and straddled down the centre of the corridor. I took the first opportunity that arose to pass, and continued on my way towards Mum's room. In passing I happened to look back at the poor old soul. Underneath her grey hair were dark warm eyes lighting up a face which was quite solemn, as she focused on the task ahead.

"Mum"!

I suddenly realised that this was my mum. She looked so old from a distance, though she was 85 years old.

"Thank goodness someone has come," she responded. "You don't know how boring it is here."

Mum had not been in the rest home long. She valued her independence, and wanted to stay in her own house as long as she could. But eventually there comes a time to surrender ones home and independence, as one becomes incapacitated through arthritis, strokes and occasional blackouts.

"Can you take me for a drive?"

"Sure Mum," I replied. "Where do you want to go?"

"Anywhere; around the block will do. Not too far in case I need to go to the toilet," Mum replied. "My bowels haven't moved today," she added.

Mum enjoyed the ride even though we just drove through some boring nearby streets. We returned to her room, where her television set was blaring, though she now didn't have the concentration to enjoy it.

"Don't turn it down," she instructed. "I have it set just right. Just leave it alone. Don't touch anything." Mum sat down in the arm chair leaving me the bed to sit on.

"So how have things been?" I asked.

"I just hate it, I just want to go," she said, quite agitated and standing back up. She started moving towards the door.

"Where are you going?" I enquired.

"I don't know," she replied, and started heading back down the hallway.

I walked with her and when we arrived at the dining area I asked her, "What is for tea tonight?"

"I don't know," she replied. "Can you look at the menu on the wall for me please?"

"Yum, you're having roast chicken and veggies."

"That sounds nice," she said. Mum commenced walking down the corridor and stopped at the television room. "Can you turn the TV up?" she asked me.

"No! No! It's loud enough" called out a number of the residents. "She has already been told no," said another.

"Come on Mum, let's go back to your room," I insisted.

We turned around and Mum stopped at the dining area. She seemed lost not knowing what she wanted to do, or where to go.

"Let me sit down, my legs are so sore," Mum said backing herself into a seat at one of the tables.

"She might as well stay," suggested one of the caregivers, who had appeared from the kitchen area. "It is almost time for tea." Mum was assisted into her seat and not long after was joined by some other elderly women.

"This is my son," she told them. "He is an accountant."

The elderly ladies said hello and went back to just sitting there saying nothing. Perhaps there was no point. There is no purpose in developing a friendship to learn a few days later that person has died.

I left Mum to have her meal and enjoy one of the few pleasures left in life. She had been a great mother; kind and thoughtful and loving to her children and grandchildren. Her life had been full, enjoying sport, painting and music, and helping others. She had travelled widely. Now she was no longer the mum I remembered. Instead, she was reduced to a frame, and a cocktail of drugs to maintain an expired body. She was ready to die.

In becoming old and wise, Mum had come to the realisation that at the end of the day what matters is your health and faith in God.

Materialistic things become meaningless as you grow older. There comes a time for all of us though, when life's journey must end. Thankfully while her life no longer had purpose, she was able to look forward with faith and an expectation of a better life to come. She died shortly after, but I will always remember my mum.

OUT OF THE MOUTH OF BABES

COLIN STRODE UP the path. He was keen to see his wife and family, but after a hard day at the office and a long walk he was also exhausted, and was looking forward to being able to collapse into a comfortable armchair. Several years ago he had learned that with young children this was impossible. This message was clearly conveyed one evening, when his young daughter stood in the middle of the newspaper he was reading. Colin needed to also consider that his wife had been home all day caring for the children, and welcomed the company of another adult, especially her husband.

Colin opened the door.

"Daddy, its Daddy," 4 year-old Emmanuel shouted as he ran to the door and put his arms around Colin's leg.

"Daddy, look what I drew at school," said excited six year-old Rachel.

Colin stroked Emmanuel on the head and picked up his daughter's drawing. "Well done, Rachel." He edged his way through the hallway to the kitchen with Emmanuel still gripping onto his leg. "How was your day dear?" he asked Jillian, who was preparing the meal.

"Not too bad Honey," she replied.

"I'm a bit later home because . . ."

"Daddy, you stink," interrupted Emmanuel.

"Exactly; I was going to say that I walked all the way home," said Colin.

"That is a long walk," replied Jillian. "You must be tired."

"Yes. From Colombo Street I took the track by the river and I found this amazing plum tree," added Colin. "There were heaps of ripe plums on it. I just wish I had time to pick them."

"Never mind perhaps another day," reassured Jillian, as she put the tea on the table.

The next day after Rachel returned home from school, Jillian suggested to the children that they go down to the river and feed the ducks. She gathered some old bread and a bucket, and they set off for the river.

"There is the track your daddy was talking about," said Jillian.

It was a dirt track winding beside the river. Weeping Willow trees lining the track draped themselves over the river. Amongst them was the rogue plum tree. It was a very secluded area with brush on the other side of the track. In the river were a number of ducks including two paradise ducks. These are a large goose-like duck endemic to New Zealand. The male has a black head and is dark grey and the female a pure white head and chestnut-coloured body. The ducks are usually in pairs and mate for life.

"You children stay here and feed the ducks," instructed Jillian. "I'm going to get some plums."

"Look! Look! Pretty ducks," shouted an excited Emmanuel.

"Paradise ducks," came a voice from above.

"You tell me what colours they are and you will get a prize," promised Rachel.

"That one black, and that one white," replied Emmanuel.

"Yes, you win the prize," declared Rachel, picking a yellow daisy from the river bank and giving it to Emmanuel.

"Mummy, I won a prize! I won a prize!" exclaimed an excited Emmanuel.

"Well done," dear called out Jillian.

"The black head duck is the daddy, when he talks he goes Zonk, Zonk," explained Rachel, as she threw the paradise ducks some bread crumbs.

"Is the white one the mummy?" asked Emmanuel.

"Yes, clever boy." Rachel said, giving him another daisy. "She has a funny voice that goes Zeek Zeek."

"Mummy, I got more prizes."

"Good boy," called Jillian.

"What other colours can you see?" asked Rachel.

"Don't know," said Emmanuel.

"Green and brown I think," Rachel said.

"What are you children doing here by the river" snapped a lady in about her mid thirties, who was walking quickly along the river track. She was obviously out for some exercise being dressed in a tee-shirt, shorts and sports shoes. "Rivers are dangerous; you could fall in and drown. You must go home," ordered the lady. The lady continued walking at pace down the track and disappeared amongst the trees lining the track.

"Do we have to go home?" asked Emmanuel.

"No silly," replied Rachel. "We can't leave mummy here on her own; she might fall in and drown."

"She was a funny walker," stated Emmanuel, as he began to imitate the lady by swinging his arms vigorously and wobbling his bottom side to side as he walked down the track a few metres.

"That looks silly," Rachel commented, and both children laughed.

They continued to feed the paradise ducks.

"Daddy said the mummy and daddy para ducks are always with each other," commented Emmanuel.

"Yes, it's good that the baby ducks will always have the same mummy and daddy," replied Rachel. "They are together for ever."

"Even when one is grumpy?" enquired Emmanuel.

"Yes and even if a prettier duck winks at one of them," said Rachel.

"Where are the babies?" asked Emmanuel.

"They don't have any yet silly," replied Rachel. "But when they do they will have both a mummy and daddy. Poor James, now only has a mummy. He has no daddy to take him to Kiwi cricket. His daddy left home."

"He must be sad," commented Emmanuel.

"Yes, he cries sometimes at school. He misses his daddy," said Rachel.

Emmanuel threw his last pieces of bread to the paradise duck saying "Your babies will be very lucky to have a mummy and daddy, and . . . ."

"What! You children still here!" It was the funny walker lady again. "You must go home. Where is your mother?"

"I'm up here," called out Jillian.

The lady somewhat stunned took time to stop walking and looked up. There was Jillian perched on a branch over the river, high up in the tree with a bucket of plums in one hand.

TAKING SHORT CUTS

"NOW SAM, DON'T forget this weekend the hedge needs trimming," reminded Sarah.

"Can't at the moment," replied Sam. "I'm off to Bunnings; there are a few things I need to get. Can you remind your son that the lawns need doing as rain is expected later this afternoon?" "That's if he decides to get up today," he sarcastically added.

Sam left the house and jumped into his prized Mercedes Kompressor. It was the best car he had ever owned and he enjoyed taking it out for drives in the weekend. He backed out the drive and set off for Bunnings. "That hedge," he thought. "It just takes so long to cut. Maybe I should invest in some electric hedge cutters while I am at Bunnings, but at the moment I don't have a few hundred dollars to spare."

It was a glorious sunny day for a drive, but this weather wouldn't last much longer before the big dark clouds arrived from the south. Sam was now driving down HoonHay Road when something caught his eye. "My gosh! What a brilliant idea," he exclaimed. He had suddenly noticed a man cutting his hedge with a rotary lawn mower. Now he had one of these. It would be rather awkward to hold on its side, but it would certainly get the job done very quickly.

After he arrived home he went straight to the tool shed. He was very excited. The lawn mower was not there. He found it on the lawn where his wife had left it for their sixteen year old son. Oliver however, not unexpectedly, was still in bed and there were no signs of life. Sam started up the lawn mower and began cutting the hedge. This was great as he sheared his way through the hedge. He was very pleased with his rapid progress. Sarah would be most impressed.

"What an absolutely brilliant idea," thought Sam. "This is really innovative; a very fast way of getting the hedge cut. Indeed it is the exact answer." By lunchtime he had cut most of the hedge and only had the woody section left. He decided to stop for lunch. At 2pm he returned to cutting the hedge. His son was still in bed.

Oliver arose shortly after, had breakfast, then went to the shed. He couldn't find the lawn mower. "Mum, where's the mower," he called.

"I've left it on the lawn for you dear," replied his mum.

Oliver went down to the lawn. He found the lawn mower caught up in some bushes and his father lying nearby badly cut and moaning loudly.

"Mum! Mum! Call an ambulance," yelled Oliver as he rushed back into the house. "It's Dad, he is hurt."

It wasn't long before Sam was rushed off to the hospital, where he received stitches for some very nasty cuts. He lay on the bed somewhat disappointed at the outcome, though was pleased to have got the hedges cut, and before it rained.

"How are you feeling?"

Sam turned around and saw a young man of about thirty standing by his bed. This was obviously one of the hospital staff, but these days it was hard to tell doctors, nurses and other staff apart. They all seemed to dress the same.

"I'm your doctor," said the young man. "You had some very nasty cuts and you will be left with some scars."

"I feel OK now," said Sam. "It all happened so quickly. One minute things were going smoothly then the next I was on the ground. But I bet you haven't seen cuts like this before?" said Sam somewhat confidently.

"Yes, they are not the normal type of cuts we see. You are right, they certainly are unique. But no, we have seen similar type cuts. In fact, today a man with the similar injuries came in from HoonHay Road," replied the doctor.

THE THING ABOUT MIRACLES

GERALD STOPPED BY his local Baptist church to drop a parcel off at the minister's office. As he entered the church he passed by the weekly prayer group sitting in a circle in the vestibule.

"We've been praying for you and your cancer every week," called out Bob who was seated in the group.

"Thank you, that's very thoughtful," replied Gerald.

"We've also been praying for safe travel for those young uns that went up to the concert in Hamilton," added Bob.

"When do they get back?" enquired Gerald.

"In about an hour," answered Bob.

Gerald delivered the parcel to the church office and returned to his van. He needed to pick up some parcels at the airport, and decided if he went now then he could also pick up the church youth group. They would be surprised, and pleased to see him as this would save them the expense of hiring a taxi.

Over the last year he had become more caring towards others as he realised his days were numbered. He had so much to do in such a short time. An X-Ray had shown what seemed to be a cancerous growth in his bowel. Gerald wasn't surprised by the X-Ray, given his age, family history, and symptoms. He had seen a specialist and was now just waiting for the results to confirm what he dreaded and suspected.

"Cheer up," he thought. "Lets just make the most of the time I have left and be more giving to others."

He hadn't been at the airport long before he noticed one of the teenagers by the airport terminal exit doorways. Gerald yelled out, "Johnny," and soon about eight teenagers appeared at his van.

"It's a miracle," announced an astonished Johnny. "When we arrived we discovered that none of us had any money for a bus or taxi."

"And not one of us had any money left on our cell phone," added Phil.

"Bummer, my battery was flat," said Jane.

"Boy, we're glad to see you," said Sarah. "Do you know we were in such a fix that we prayed, then wow! Just like that, you turn up; hallelujah!"

"Cool—a miracle," said someone else in the group.

The teenagers hoped into the van, and Gerald headed back to the church to drop them off.

"So did you have a good concert?" asked Gerald.

"It was amazing, real cool," replied Sarah.

"Oh, um Johnny, how are your parents?" asked Gerald.

Johnny was the son of Gerald's doctor. His parents were on an overseas trip through Europe.

"My parents are um currently in Paris, and having a great time. It's good to see Dad getting away from his work; he just never stops," Johnny added. "You know, on the day they left to go, Dad was in such a flap; so much unfinished business. Mum had to take him in hand. Oh!" Johnny reached deep down into his pocket and pulled out an envelope. "On the day my dad left, he asked me to give you this. Sorry, I clearly forgot," apologised Johnny.

Gerald took the envelope and put it on the dashboard. "So are they enjoying Paris?" asked Gerald.

"They love it, and yesterday they saw the Mona Lisa. Quite a small painting they said, and crowds of people around it," added Johnny.

"Looks like we are here," advised Gerald, as they arrived at the church.

Without even a thank you, the teenagers leaped out of the van and made their way to the church. Gerald leaned back on his seat.

"Teenagers!" he exclaimed. "Not a worry in the world. Guess I was once like that." He was about to drive off when he remembered the envelope on the dashboard. Gerald ripped open the envelope and unfolded the letter.

"Gerald," it began. "The first X-Ray indicated a growth in your bowel, which clearly looked to be cancer. I can't explain this, but the second X-Ray showed your bowel to be clear, and all the other tests confirm you do not have cancer."

"Now that is a miracle," thought Gerald.

AUCKLAND OR BUST

"DO YOU KNOW over the last five years, we have been to Australia three times, and the last time I saw Auckland was as a teenager about thirty years ago."

"So you would have preferred to go to Auckland rather than the Gold coast of Australia Dan, is that what your saying?"

"No, not exactly, but they do say you should see your own country first, and I would like to go to Auckland, even if it was just for a night."

"Well, I'm sorry to inform you dear, but this plane is heading for Coolangatta, Australia."

The plane touched down at Coolangatta and Dan and Alice took a shuttle to their beachfront hotel.

The next day they sunbathed on the golden beach and bathed in the warm water.

"You don't get glorious weather like this in Auckland," Alice remarked.

"I wouldn't know," mumbled Dan.

Later in the day they walked to Tweeds Head shopping area, which happened to be across the road.

"Now that's something you can't do in New Zealand," commented Alice. "Coolangatta is in the State of Queensland, yet the other side of this road is Tweeds Head and the State of New South Wales."

Over the remaining days they mixed bush walks with exploring Broad Beach, Surfers Paradise and other beautiful parts of the Gold Coast. They enjoyed watching the various indigenous Australian parrots like the small colourful Lorikeets and large white Cockatoos perched in the trees. The week went very quickly and both Alice and Dan had a wonderful time and displayed a nice sun tan.

"Now here is your ticket for the return flight back to New Zealand Dan," said Alice. "Oh, in case you're wondering, the ticket says for destination 'Christchurch', and not Auckland."

"Very funny," responded Dan, as they boarded their flight.

It didn't seem long before they were close to landing at Christchurch.

"Please take your seats, fasten your safety belts, and prepare for landing at Christchurch airport," came an announcement over the plane intercom.

"Christchurch," Alice repeated sarcastically to Dan.

The plane descended and Dan listened to hear the wheels touch the tarmac. Suddenly, the plane sped up and rose at a steep angle. People gripped their seats hoping the plane would gain sufficient clearance of the trees on the other side of the runway.

"Sorry folks," came the pilot's voice over the intercom. "Couldn't see the runway due to fog. We'll try again from a different approach."

The plane again descended and Dan waited to hear the safe sound of the wheels greeting the runway. Suddenly, the plane again rose steeply and once again anxiety took hold. This was the type of stuff you watched on television programmes about plane crashes.

"Sorry folks, there's too much fog, we will now be landing at Auckland where the airline will put you up for the night,"

"Auckland," Dan repeated sarcastically.

"Did you hear? Auckland."

CAUGHT IN THE ACT

MARK AND RYAN battled their way through the street market. It was crowded with people, mostly out to find a bargain or two. The road, alongside the market was also very busy with a constant flow of traffic. A Tuk-Tuk buzzed past. The two tourists seated in the back held handkerchiefs over their mouths and noses to filter out the petrol fumes of passing vehicles.

"Bad choice of transport for these polluted Bangkok streets," commented Mark.

"Bloody must be 35degrees," said Ryan wiping the sweat from his forehead.

"You'll get used to it," reassured twenty-year old Mark. "I did, when I first came here with Dad."

Ryan, who was nineteen and on his first overseas trip, stopped to look at a padded black wind-jacket with Ferrari written in red across the back.

"Wow, I really like that jacket," declared Ryan.

"Cheap, 500 baht," yelled out the stall owner.

"No, too much," Ryan replied.

"400 baht," suggested the stall owner.

"Leave it," instructed Mark. "The market will still be here when we get back."

They continued on their way through the market.

"How much you wanta pay?" called out the stall owner.

Ryan hesitated.

"Can sell you cheaper," he added.

"Come on," ordered Mark.

Ryan reluctantly moved ahead. He really wanted to buy that jacket. They continued to walk through the market, looking, but not expressing too much interest lest another stall owner engage them in negotiation.

"So, how far away is this computer place?" asked Ryan, still feeling the heat and who now held a sweat sodden handkerchief.

"We follow the market up the road as far as you can see, then we turn around the corner. Not too far away then," explained Mark.

"What stuff does this place sell?" Ryan asked.

"Everything, it's cool," informed Mark. "Even pirated computer programmes. Cheap-as; like $5."

"Man, that's wicked," replied Ryan.

"I'm really looking forward to getting a lot of cheap software," added Mark.

"Buying pirated stuff, imitation brands; it is all theft," stated a concerned Ryan. "You don't want to end up in a Thai prison."

"It is a crime if you sell it," replied Mark. "But if it is for your own use it's OK."

"So it's OK to receive stolen property then?" asked Ryan. "Are you really happy depriving the game-makers of their livelihood?"

"Look, they're only getting a small part of the sale price anyway," responded Mark. "It's the middlemen and retailers who get most of the sale price. Anyhow, it's my call and I'm buying this software whether you like it or not."

"Well I won't be," stated an adamant Ryan.

They continued walking down the street and crossed over the road to the computer place. It was enormous with floor upon floor of everything. There was a countless selection of electronic equipment. This included computer hardware and accessories, Xboxes, play stations, security cameras, software and much, much more.

"I'm off to buy some software. I'll meet you here by the escalator in half an hour," Mark said.

Mark headed towards some software sellers, whereas Ryan took the escalator up to a higher level to find some electronic equipment he was interested in buying.

At the software counter a male vendor looked quite agitated. He was quickly moving stuff off the shelf into boxes. His female colleague was also quite anxious. She was leaning across the counter surreptitiously slipping a customer some purchased software. Mark went up to the counter.

"Do you have . . . ."

"Not now," interrupted the vendor. "Come back twenty minutes. Man has come back."

"What man?" asked Mark.

"Fat man; there in brown shirt. He wants close us down. Go now. Come later; cheap software."

Mark headed off to look at other computer parts.

About twenty minutes later, Ryan returned to the escalator and waited for Mark. He hadn't been there long when a large man in a brown shirt approached him.

"So where are you from?" he enquired.

"New Zealand," Ryan replied.

". . . . and you came here to buy computer parts, cheap; software maybe?" he added.

"Just some controllers for my Xbox," replied Ryan. "I don't want anything that's pirated."

"Show me what you bought?" asked the fat man.

Ryan opened his plastic bag and showed him the controllers.

"Good choice," replied the fat man and walked away.

"Very strange," Ryan thought. "Could this man be checking for pirated goods? Mark better be careful or he might be in big trouble. Thai prisons are not nice."

The fat man started to walk towards the software vendors stall. To Ryan's horror, Mark suddenly appeared and was walking in the direction of the fat man. It was too late as the fat man had seen Mark and engaged him in conversation. Then he saw the fat man look in Mark's plastic bag.

Suddenly, a number of high school students appeared obscuring Ryan's view. When the students had moved on, both Mark and the fat man had disappeared.

"Oh dear, what will I tell Mark's parents," thought Ryan thinking the worst.

"Well, are you ready to go?" Ryan turned around. It was Mark.

"What happened, did you get nicked for pirated software?" asked Ryan.

"No," replied Mark. "I didn't buy any."

"You didn't!" responded Ryan somewhat aghast.

They returned to the street market where Ryan purchased his Ferrari jacket for 150 baht.

"Well, are you satisfied now Ryan, with your imitation formula one jacket?" Mark asked.

DAD

"HELLO HOW IS everyone?"

Gregory announced his presence as he bounced through the door. His elderly parents were stooped over a cup of tea. They looked somewhat subdued.

"What's up?" enquired a now concerned Gregory.

Mum slowly looked up and towards her husband. Dad then turned towards Gregory. His father cleared his throat then cleared it again and responded. "Er not that good."

"You need to tell him. Bob, tell him," interrupted his mum.

"I er, went to the doctor yesterday. I er; I am not well"

"It's very serious," interrupted Mum. "Tell him."

"I . . . I have prostate cancer. Guess I won't make a hundred after all. The doctor gave me two years, as it has already spread to the bones."

His seventy-six year old dad looked sad; his eyes watery. He surreptitiously ran his arm across his face to stop a tear rolling down his cheek. "So, life has come to this," Dad added, looking away to hide new tears forming around both eyes.

"I'm sorry," replied a stunned Gregory. "I really just don't know what to say. You've always been so fit and healthy. I just don't understand how you can suddenly get cancer. Why wasn't this picked up by the doctor earlier? What a bombshell. I think I will have a cup of tea too; yes I will."

The weeks and months passed, and over this period Dad received radiation treatment and drugs to destroy the cancer. But radiation is accumulative and there came a time when he reached the maximum amount of radiation his body could safely hold. After this treatment was stopped, the cancer spread and the pain intensified. The dosage of morphine was accordingly increased and with it came all the side effects. But this was only the start to his demise. To think that once he was a manager who controlled a large organisation. Now, as he became increasingly incapacitated, he didn't even have much control over his own life. What he had was increasingly diminishing.

Now dependent on drugs and nurses, he had only self respect left. This too was stripped away as a nurse would come to shower him. Then when it seemed he had no self respect left to take, he was removed from his castle to spend his last days in a hospice. Even here the few pleasures left like a television set were short-lived, as he was now too weak to sit up and concentrate. The television was eventually taken from his room.

Gregory walked into the hospice. His father was lying on the bed, and only had a few days to live. He looked terrible. His once bouncy red hair was flat and grey. Gregory at first hoped he had walked into the wrong room. This gaunt elderly prostrate man surely could not be his father. It certainly didn't look like him. Beside the bed were his sister and mother. They were talking and seemed oblivious of Dad lying there in front of them. His sister looked up as he walked into the room.

"Good to see you," said his sister.

"How is he?" Gregory asked.

"In and out of consciousness," replied his sister.

"Maybe he would like a drink of water," suggested Gregory eying the glass of water on the bedside table.

"No, no, he can't take anything through his mouth now," stated Mum.

"To give him water you have to wet the cotton bud, and put it in his mouth," advised his sister.

"For goodness sake, has his life come to this?" Gregory was very angry. "We are kinder to our animals and save them all this suffering." He was now more than ever persuaded by the euthanasia arguments.

"Shush! Your dad can hear every word," reminded Mum, who seemed very well composed, given that this was her lifetime partner dying before her eyes.

"Well, I really feel for Dad. Once he was an icon and had control over his life, but now he has nothing. Everything is now in God's hands."

"Gregory, our lives are always in God's hand, even when we think we are in control," informed Mum.

THE COIN

PHILIP BENT DOWN to pick up the book he had dropped on the floor.

"Ouch!"

Something in his back pocket was pressing hard against his bottom. Philip reached his hand down deep into his back pocket. His fingers touched something like a coin.

"Two dollars," he thought. This was a lot of money for an eleven year old. Philip managed to curl his fingers around it and slide it up and out of the pocket. He checked to confirm it was two dollars. No, this was not a two dollar coin. It was a coin he had never seen before.

"Granddad, what is this coin?" asked Philip. Granddad glanced up from his newspaper.

"Probably ten cents," he replied, retreating back behind the newspaper.

"No Granddad, this is a golden colour and it is much heavier than a two dollar coin. It has a soldier on a horse."

"Where? Let me see?" responded Granddad, suddenly throwing down the newspaper and expressing a lot of interest. "Where did you find it?"

"It was in the pocket of these jeans Grandma got me from the op shop," replied Philip.

"This is not a two dollar coin," stated Granddad.

"I know that," interjected Philip sadly.

"It's a gold sovereign and it's worth hundreds of dollars," continued Granddad.

"Stop tricking," said Philip. "Grandma said it was naughty to tell lies."

"No seriously, it's true," reassured Granddad. "Let me tell you a story." Philip liked Granddad's stories. He didn't hesitate to perch himself next to Granddad on the sofa. Granddad removed his glasses and began his story.

"Many years ago, when I was a lad, a wee bit older than you, I found a half gold sovereign. Our family was poor, so my dad took the half sovereign to pay for the family needs."

"Will Dad take my sovereign?" questioned a concerned Philip.

"I doubt it," replied Granddad. "Your family isn't poor. I think your dad would like you to put it somewhere safe."

"What was your half sovereign worth?" asked Philip.

"Probably only half of what your sovereign would have been worth. It may have been worth now about one hundred dollars. Oh, yes, I forgot to tell you how I found it." At times Granddad did get distracted and lose his train of thought.

"How did you find it Granddad?"

"Oh yes. Well, as I said we were very poor and we lived in a very old house. We had no carpet—just floor boards. Some had holes where the knots had been. One day I dropped a threepence I had earned for cutting the next door neighbour's lawn. Do you know what a threepence is?"

"Of course I do, Granddad. They are a small silver coin. I have these in my coin collection."

"Anyhow, it fell on to the floor and rolled across and disappeared down a hole in the floor."

"You must have been angry, Granddad."

"Yes, I was Philip. I had worked hard for that threepence. I was determined I was going to get it back. With a hammer I pulled up the floorboard."

"Oh, what did your dad say? Did you get into big trouble?"

"No, he didn't know."

"And you found the half sovereign Granddad?"

"Yes, and my threepence of course."

"What did you do with the threepence?"

"I put it somewhere safe and it became my lucky threepence," replied Granddad. "In fact, you know, I believe I still have it tucked away in one of my drawers."

"Can I see it?" asked Philip who seemed rather excited.

"It's only a threepence," Granddad replied. "Just like those in your collection of threepences and besides a threepence today wouldn't even buy a lolly."

"Please can I see your lucky threepence," insisted Philip.

"Alright then," said Granddad easing himself up from his seat.

Granddad disappeared into his bedroom and sometime later came out with an old matchbox. He slid the drawer of the box open and there embedded amongst cotton wool was a shiny threepence.

"Granddad!" exclaimed Philip, after examining the coin. "Your dad took your half sovereign worth $100, but do you know this threepence may be worth a thousand."

"Very funny," responded Granddad. "This is just a common old New Zealand threepence."

"Yes, but it is 1935, a very rare threepence," replied an excited Philip.

TAKING FLIGHT

"MATHEW WATSON, DOCTOR Dobson," said the tall grey-headed 52 year old man at the reception desk.

The receptionist scrolled down her computer screen.

"Five-thirty; take a seat Mr Watson."

Mathew looked across at the choice of seating available. On his left was a teenage girl holding a handkerchief and occasionally sneezing into it. He would definitely sit well away from her. Mathew decided to isolate himself in one corner of the room. In two weeks time he and his wife Amy were off for a week in Melbourne. He certainly didn't want to catch anything from any of the four patients sitting in the reception area.

Doctor Dobson walked into reception. Mathew moved forward to get up. "That's good he's right on time for once," he thought.

"Cynthia Brown," Doctor Dobson called out.

A thin elderly lady manoeuvred to the edge of her seat and, with the aid of a walking stick and a great deal of effort, slowly rose to her feet. Then after shuffling herself into position to get good balance, waddled behind the doctor to his examination room.

Mathew relaxed back sinking into his seat somewhat disappointed that once again his doctor was running late. There was a newspaper on the small table in front of him so he leaned forward and grabbed it. This should tide over ten minutes of waiting time. Then in frustration he placed the newspaper back on the table as he realised he didn't have his glasses. Mathew had not had glasses for long, but he hated them and could never remember where he left them; needing glasses was very frustrating. He decided to just sit back and think about the trip to Melbourne in two weeks time. Both he and Amy, his wife, were looking forward to going to his nephew's wedding, riding around Melbourne on the trams, and visiting Victoria Market.

He was fed up and needed a break. Since September last year Christchurch had been rocked by over 5000 earthquakes or aftershocks. Twenty-six had been Richter scale 5 or greater. Mathew just wanted out; a time to get away and get his life back together.

The elderly lady was back; this time slowly hobbling over to the reception counter to pay her account. This poor old soul looked like she was on her last legs.

"Mr Watson," a voice called out

Mathew jumped up and followed the doctor into his room.

"So what's the problem?" asked Dr Dobson.

"For the last two nights I have been extremely uncomfortable when lying down in bed; it seems to hurt whatever position I am in. It's probably really nothing, but I thought I should check it out."

"So where does it hurt?" asked the doctor.

"This might seem silly, but I'm not sure; it's everywhere around my chest," replied Mathew.

The doctor started prodding Mathew's back, but the area of pain could not be located. Mathew began to feel like a hypochondriac, and was close to saying "just forget it." The doctor got out his stethoscope.

"Breathe in, out, in, out," he instructed. "The right lung is not performing at all well," the doctor commented. He hesitated. "Er sorry, but you're off to hospital. I will call an ambulance."

"No need for that," said Mathew somewhat stunned. "I have my car just outside."

"You're going in an ambulance," repeated the doctor in a firmer voice.

Shortly after, the ambulance arrived. The ambulance driver walked into the health centre.

"Well, where is the patient?" he asked.

"I'm it," replied Mathew.

"You!"

"Yes, I'm surprised too," replied Mathew. "Can I ride in the front?"

"No, you have to get in the back," instructed the driver. Once in the back of the ambulance Mathew had his pulse and blood pressure taken and had an oxygen mask put over his nose. When they arrived at the hospital Mathew was told he needed to wait till they got a wheel chair.

"Hey, it's only my lungs, I am quite capable of walking," stated Mathew.

"Sorry, but everyone enters accident and emergency in a wheel chair," said the driver.

On entering the hospital Mathew had to first answer some questions before being directed to a bed. The nurse connected him up to an oxygen monitor and attached a pulse monitor to his finger. Shortly after a blood sample was taken and he was taken for a chest X-Ray.

Mathew was lying on the bed when Amy his wife appeared.

"So what's the story you old goat. You're not going to die on me just yet?" she asked. "Your oxygen level is low at 85 and your blood pressure is high. Have they found out what's wrong?"

Before Mathew could answer a doctor appeared on the scene and asked Mathew about the symptoms. She was a young lady who couldn't have been much older than 25.

"Have you recently had a virus?"

"No," answered Mathew.

"Been on a long trip in a plane recently?"

"No."

The doctor was quite perplexed, and as suddenly as she appeared; she disappeared.

"Silly old goat. Bit of an enigma aren't you?" commented Amy sarcastically. "That lovely young doctor is now all confused. Soon you'll have the whole hospital running around trying to solve your problem."

Shortly after, the original doctor, plus another doctor, and an ultra sound machine arrived. One doctor started moving the ultra sound probe over the lungs and heart.

"A wee bit of fluid around the heart, but not enough to account for the symptoms," he commented. The nurse came over with the blood test results. "Mm! You have an infection in your lungs—pneumonia," informed the male doctor. "I will put you on antibiotics and if your oxygen levels get back to an acceptable level you won't have to spend the night."

Mathew was fortunately able to go home that night and was given a week's supply of antibiotics.

"Well, I'm still going to Melbourne in one week's time," declared a determined Mathew. He had completed his week's course of antibiotics, and could now sleep comfortably at night except for the tooth ache. This excruciating pain had commenced almost immediately he had completed the course of drugs. So now it was a case of having to go to the dentist.

Mathew sat in the reception area of the dental clinic. He looked on the table but there was no newspaper, and this time he had his glasses. All he could see were girly magazines. He again used the time to think about Melbourne, the warmer climate and of course the wedding.

"The dentist will see you now," said the nurse.

After a careful check up the dentist concluded:

"I can give you a temporary filling to tide you over the Melbourne trip, but I am afraid the tooth will have to come out, or the nerve removed."

Mathew left with a temporary filling and the satisfaction that nothing now could stand in the way of their Melbourne trip in two days time. Nothing; absolutely nothing now could stop him.

The remaining days went fast without further incidents. Mathew didn't break a leg, or catch influenza. He was extremely careful where he went and what he did. It didn't seem long before the big day arrived and Amy and Mathew were at the airport.

"Flights delayed till 4.50pm," Amy pointed out.

"You know when I first booked several months ago this started off as a morning flight. Now it keeps getting made later and later," stated Mathew.

At 4.50pm the flight was delayed again; now to 6.15pm. At about 6.00pm there was an announcement.

"All those on flight 212 to Melbourne please report to the counter, this flight has been cancelled."

ZAMBIA LAND OF HOPE

THE TRUCK CRAWLED out of the compound. Spending a night here in Lusaka—the capital of Zambia had been a unique but scary experience, despite the compound being well fortified by two-metre high concrete block walls. Beyond these walls was a ghetto and an area covered in rubbish. This ghetto was inhabited by people who had probably once been attracted to the big city, with its electricity, water on tap, and materialistic comforts. Instead, many had found unemployment, prostitution, drugs, crime, and poverty.

As the truck pulled out onto the shingle roadway, we encountered about twenty ghetto children kicking a soccer ball. Their play area—the rubbish dump; a minefield to their bare feet. They stopped playing and turned to look in our direction as we passed by on the back of the truck. In their envious eyes we were millionaires.

The truck left the shingle road and turned onto the main road heading towards town. This was sealed though poorly maintained.

"Sorry folks, but we have to first get supplies at the supermarket," informed Mathew, the group's leader. This was not the first time Mathew had taken a voluntary work group of about a dozen church folk to carry out repairs at the missionary hospital in Luampa. "I think you will all enjoy the stop anyway. It's next to a market. Now please, I will need three of you to accompany me in getting the supplies from the supermarket. A further three I need to stay on the back of the truck to ensure nothing walks and . . ."

"Walks . . . ? What do you mean *walks*?" interrupted Frank, one of the volunteers.

"At the supermarket car park, we'll need to look out for wandering hands; you'll see," replied Mathew. "Now where was I? Ah, yes; the remaining five can go to the market, but please don't take too long as others might want to go as well."

"Bags going to the market," declared Frank, who now looked happier.

Frank was a partly grey haired married man of about 45. In the ten years I had known him, he never looked to be a person who was content with life, despite having a nice family, house, boat, and plenty of money. He had also travelled extensively around the world. Next to him, I looked a scruff in my old worn tee-shirt and stained jeans. My dress code, though, was consistent with most of my fellow travellers. Frank looked out of place dress-wise. He had told others in our group that he had purchased the blue, silk shirt he was wearing from Italy and it had some fancy label. His trendy shorts had come from Harrods in England.

The truck pulled slowly into the supermarket car park. Immediately we were inundated by a gang of Zambian nationals, some bearing items for sale, while others surreptitiously pressed and passed their hands over the suitcases set around the internal perimeter of the truck decking. I remained with two other members of our party guarding the items, which thankfully had been deliberately secured on the back of the truck.

About 15 minutes later, Mathew returned with the groceries. These were placed well back in the covered area of the truck, well away from wandering hands. Mathew and his grocery group then left to explore the market, while we waited for Frank and the others to return. Eventually we were also able to satisfy our own curiosity. The market was amazing; everything being so cheap. There were various carved wooden items, clothing, and even items such as toy cars made from wire. I purchased a carved wooden plaque in the shape of Africa, then returned to the truck.

"Look at this!" said an excited Frank. "This is a chess set carved out of marble and African jade . . . and here look!" He reached into a large plastic bag and pulled out a motorbike made out of wire, some carved wooden bowls and a carved Africa. This was similar to mine, but with a carved elephant and hippo included in the design. "Look at the craftsmanship; the hours of work that would have been involved," he added.

"So you've decided to do all your shopping at the start of the trip," commented one of the women in our group.

"Are you kidding, I've only just started," replied an excited Frank.

The truck lurched forward as we set off for Luampa in the far north. Soon we reached the main highway and headed north dodging the occasional pothole. Luampa is close to the Kalahari Desert. The hospital and staff houses are encircled by villages and yellow sand. This would be our place of work and home for the next six weeks.

In contrast to Lusaka, there was no fortification between the staff houses and the surrounding villages. These too were poor people, but were not perceived as a threat. While they didn't have the luxuries of running water, a sewerage system and electric power, they were content with their self sufficiency in food and water. The hospital and staff houses had water, electricity and a sewerage system, as a result of a water tower, diesel generator and sewerage pond.

As the truck pulled up to the staff houses, we were greeted like royalty. A large number of villagers had assembled. They were very excited to see us. Their large happy smiles were accentuated by white teeth contrasted against their black skins. The missionary doctors and nurses were also pleased to see fresh faces and to receive well needed supplies. As we learned, the missionaries are kept very busy in running the hospital. They service a wide catchment where there are few if any doctors—otherwise just witch doctors. Life is hard for the Zambian people with a life expectancy of about 35years largely due to aids, malaria and bilharzia.

"The place doesn't seem to have changed since two years ago when I was last here," commented Mathew.

"Not so," responded an excited doctor. "The people now have a well. This should see a reduction in the cases of Bilharzia. We are extremely pleased."

"Bilharzia"! I repeated looking somewhat puzzled.

Mathew turned to me and explained. "It's a fatal illness caused by a microscopic worm carried by snails in the river. The worm can penetrate the skin and destroy the liver."

"But with the right drugs they can be treated successfully," added the doctor. "The drugs are very expensive though," he added.

". . . . and malaria?" asked one of the woman in our group looking towards the doctor.

"Still as bad as last time you were here Mathew. Fortunately, we still have a drug that works which the malaria hasn't become resistant to. The problem is that the nationals use bundles of elephant grass to roof their brick houses. The mosquitoes can get into the houses under the elephant grass, and as they cannot afford mosquito nets, they get bitten and die if not treated."

"What about aids?" enquired a 35 year old man standing next to me.

". . . . and as for aids, this has got worse. A lot of the problem is culture."

"What do you mean?" I asked.

"Well, the custom is that you buy your wife, but how many young men can afford to pay a cow or two? So what results is a lot of unprotected premarital sex."

"If the girl gets pregnant?" questioned Frank.

"A woman with a child is more valuable and worth more cows," replied the doctor.

Mathew and the missionaries parted and Mathew rallied the group together directing them to their new dwellings. I was placed in the same house as Frank and five other males. Frank seemed to be back to his sad old self.

"We seem to be out in the wop wops. There are no shops or markets," he moaned.

"I wouldn't be too sure about that," said the oldest in the group, a fifty year old man who had been here before. "There is a marketplace, and if you want to buy a bow and arrows, wooden, flax or root woven plates and bowls then you can find the people who make these in the various villages. But you don't really need to look for them; they'll turn up at our door anyway."

"Really," said Frank with his eyes lighting up.

Over the next weeks Frank took advantage of the villagers who visited and brought many things to sell. Questions were raised on how he would circumvent airline weight restrictions. He had certainly purchased a lot of souvenirs. In contrast, I spent very little, preferring instead to meet the Zambians and understand their culture.

The days and nights passed quickly, as we went about carrying out repairs to the hospital and mixing with the villagers. At night we certainly knew it was winter as we tried to keep warm in our sleeping bags under our mosquito nets. At 7.30am at prayer meetings, we assembled outside around a blazing fire in order to keep from freezing. By 10.30 temperatures had rocketed to as high as 48 degrees celsius under a full sun. It was a warm bright sun that seemed to lack the burning sensation one became accustomed to in New Zealand.

"Great! It's Saturday, a free day," I declared.

"Do you want to come with me to the local market?" offered Frank.

"Not today," I replied. "Sullivan, the 65 year-old Zambian who has been assisting me with the painting of the dispensary, has invited me to his house." I walked with Frank over the soft yellow sand then over a foot-worn track cutting its way through tall elephant grass. Near the market we parted. I headed towards the village where Sullivan lived. Sullivan was waiting with his 26year-old wife, whom he had bought for two cows.

"She's so young," I whispered to Sullivan. "Who provides for her and her children when you die?"

"My brother. She will become his wife."

We went inside to his small humble dwelling. Like the other houses in the various villages, there was no electricity, no water and no sewerage services. The house was small comprising three small rooms. We sat down at the table.

"Here," he said, placing two small bottles of soft drink in front of me. I knew each bottle cost one dollar and that one dollar was his hourly wage rate.

"Just one bottle," I said, pushing the other to one side. I felt somewhat flattered, but also embarrassed at his generosity.

He put a glass in front of me.

"Three glasses," I instructed.

He returned with another glass and sat down at the table.

"Three glasses," I repeated looking towards his wife who was standing nearby.

Sullivan hesitated for four or five seconds, then slowly and reluctantly arose from the table returning with another glass. I filled the three glasses and passed his wife a glass. She looked towards Sullivan and he nodded.

Frank was pleased to see me when I got back. He looked very pleased with himself. "I found some beautiful material at the market.

It's the material the women here use for their wrap around long dresses. My wife will be pleased," he added.

"Well, I also had a great time; a cultural experience," I replied.

The day finally arrived when we sadly had to pack our suitcases in preparation for our departure. Mine was somewhat lighter, as I had given away most of my clothes. I took my case to the truck and had just placed it on the deck when a voice called out, "Well! First time; what did you think?" I turned around; it was Mathew.

"I will certainly miss this place," I began. "It is just so amazing. This is a subsistence culture—they don't have power, water or electrical services. There are no transistor radios, television sets, torches, cars, or even motor bikes. In fact they have nothing and death is always knocking at the door. I just don't understand it. All they are left with is hope; yet they are happy,"

"And yet, Frank has everything and is seldom happy," added Mathew.

THE INTERVIEW

PETER HAD ARRIVED for his job interview ten minutes early.

"Take a seat," said the receptionist directing him to a couch by the window.

Peter sat down, and spent the first five minutes checking his burgundy tie, picking fluff off his blue pin-striped suit and running a comb through his fine, black hair. From his studies he knew that first impressions would influence how he was perceived.

He suddenly caught sight of a selection of magazines lying at the end of the brown, vinyl couch. "Reading a magazine could be good for my nerves," he thought, as he fingered his way through the selection. He picked up the best of a poor choice of mostly girly magazines, and began to flick his way through the pages. Every now and again he surreptitiously glanced across at the young receptionist. My, she was a bit of all right. Her shoulder length blond hair together with blue eyes and superb facial features made her a sight to behold.

Peter's persistent glances in her direction were well rewarded when she rose to place papers into the filing cabinet at the end of the counter. Her short tight leather dress exposed not only a pair of shapely legs but also a slim well-proportioned figure.

His view was momentarily interrupted when a well dressed young man awkwardly emerged from one of the nearby rooms and stormed past. His speedy departure together with a flushed complexion suggested he may have endured a torturous interrogation for the same job.

"Mr Matthews?"

Peter looked up to meet the brown eyes of a tall, slim, sprightly man of about forty.

"Mr Matthews, I'm Bob; Bob Green."

Peter quickly rose, ensuring Bob received a firm hand shake. His father had often told him that a firm shake showed strength of character.

"Please come this way," directed Bob, ushering Peter into a musty wood panelled office. Behind a large wooden desk slouched a grey-headed conservatively-dressed man. His lined forehead and yellow parched skin betrayed an age of at least sixty.

"Mr Waring," said the elderly man rising slightly and extending his arm across the desk.

"And this is Miss Webb," he added, redirecting Peter's attention to a woman of about thirty-five seated by the wall.

Peter smiled with a "Hi". He was not accustomed to shaking a woman's hand, so he didn't. Miss Webb returned a forced smile.

Bob had meanwhile sat down on a seat on the other side of Mr Waring. This left Peter with the seat that faced the interview panel. Mr Waring had re-established himself on his comfortable swivel chair and almost immediately started taking notes on the paper in front of him.

"You're twenty-five," stated Bob Green, hardly giving Peter a chance to settle in his seat.

"Yes."

"When you applied for a job in this company did you read the job description and person specification?"

"Yes."

Mr Green paused to ensure some long strands of his hair still traversed the bald central area of his head before remarking; "So then, you will know all about the job?"

"No, no! I only know what I read in the job description and what I learned from subsequent phone enquiries," retorted Peter shuffling in his seat. "But perhaps you can give me further background knowledge of the job," added Peter.

Peter had now had six unsuccessful job interviews over the last two months and had learned that it was paramount to show an interest in the job.

Mr Green appeared pleased with this response. He leaned back in his seat and began what seemed a long painful description of the job and the company. Mr Waring sat back seeming to share a similar passion for the organisation, and occasionally he would nod in agreement. Peter tried to look interested, well aware that he was being observed.

As Mr Green continued to explain the job, Miss Webb continued to become more restless in her seat. It was obvious she was eager for the interview to proceed and did not share the same passion. Finally, she found an opportunity to put her questions to Peter.

"Do you really think you are sufficiently qualified to do this job? Our engineers, you know, usually have degrees and you, you only have a diploma."

Miss Webb sat back quite satisfied at her provocative question.

Peter felt somewhat offended but tried to remain composed. He had studied hard for his qualification. Grasping his seat, he straightened up. Looking Miss Webb in the eyes he calmly replied,

"Yes, I don't have a degree, but I do have relevant experience."

Miss Webb sat forward in her seat somewhat surprised by the response. She tugged at the hem of her red dress which was exposing a little too much leg for her liking.

"And what experience do you consider to be relevant?" she continued.

Peter described the various jobs he had done and explained how these related to the job vacancy. At least Mr Waring now looked interested and was sitting back in his chair. Peter however wondered whether this was one of those job interviews where they had already decided on the successful applicant. He had been around long enough to know that it was often not the best applicant who got the job, and besides, as an outsider his chances were at best slim. Besides he was being given the third degree.

Miss Webb sat back in her seat, crossing her legs and listening to Peter's reply. At one stage she ran her fingers through her short curly brown hair, until she remembered where she was, and with a sudden move jerked herself into a more upright position in her seat.

"What do you consider are your weaknesses?" interrupted Mr Green, who had heard enough about Peter's experiences.

"Beg your pardon?" responded Peter somewhat caught off-guard.

"Weaknesses, you know—like some people might be good at organising but not good at listening. What are you not good at?" enquired Mr Green.

"Oh, um, well actually I am a very enthusiastic person and at times this can be a weakness," replied Peter.

"I would have thought it to be more a strength," retorted Mr Green.

Before Bob could ask another question, Mr Waring reminded everyone of his presence by loudly clearing his throat.

"Why have you been in your current job for quite some time without promotion?" he asked.

Peter turned his head slowly towards Mr Waring. It was now clear to him that they had someone else jacked up for the job. He was obviously there just to make up the numbers so they could support their appointment.

"Unfortunately the company I work for is small with few opportunities in the way of promotion, unless I am prepared to move out of Christchurch. Frankly, I prefer to stay in Christchurch."

Mr Waring quickly cast glances in the directions of Mr Green and Miss Webb, then refocused on Peter. There was silence in the room. Mr Waring adjusted his glasses, but said nothing.

"The silence technique," Peter thought. He had encountered this before and knew how to handle it.

"I take it that promotion opportunities are considerably better in your organisation?" he enquired.

"Er, yes, of course," replied a surprised Mr Waring.

Peter felt pleased with his overall handling of the interview. An hour was a long time to be barraged by questions, trying to remain composed and appearing to look interested. The interview now seemed to be drawing to an end. Peter sensed from the questions that had been asked, that this vacancy might already have been filled. This interview he concluded would have to be put down to being a learning experience.

"Any more questions Bob?" asked Mr Waring.

"No, I'm happy," replied Mr Green.

"And you Sarah?" addressing Miss Webb.

"OK," answered Miss Webb with a relaxed smile.

Mr Waring then turned towards Peter, at the same time adjusting his glasses.

"Well, do you want the job?"

"Beg your pardon?" exclaimed Peter.

"Do you want the job?"

THE BIG DUMP

"DO YOU THINK the weatherman will be right?" asked Roger, as he lay in bed next to Sharon.

"It was hailing before, but I can't hear anything now," replied Sharon.

"When it snows it is very quiet; it can be so eerie," commented Roger. "What I do know is that it has got a lot colder," he said pulling the duvet over his shoulders.

The next morning Roger peeped out through the curtains.

"Oh my, gosh!" he exclaimed.

"Has it snowed?" asked Sharon still trying to keep warm in bed by pulling more of the blankets over on to her side.

"That's an understatement," stated Roger. "But it does look so beautiful with lots of little snow flakes floating down and decorating the deciduous trees. A bit like a mystical land; like something out of a children's story book."

"Snow is beautiful and will be fun for the kids, but you may have a few jobs to do to day, like shovelling snow off the path," pointed out Sharon.

Roger went outside. It was the biggest snow dump he had ever seen. It soon became apparent that he would have more than shovelling snow to do. A tree had fallen with the weight of the snow. Around him the silence of the snow falling was broken by the occasional sound of a tree falling from the hillside above. Roger climbed over a fallen tree with rake in hand. He was determined to prevent any more of his trees from falling. The snowflakes fell onto his face obscuring his vision, while the cold air burned his finger tips. He trudged his way through the snow then carefully climbed up the snow caked steps to the garden above. Once he had reached the garden he dropped down into the bushy area of the garden and commenced shaking the trees with the rake. The trees responded by showering Roger with clumps of snow that had been weighing their branches down. Some trees had been close to toppling over. Now they were able to be relieved of their burden and once again stand tall.

It wasn't long before Roger couldn't feel his fingers and he was wet and cold. He returned to the steps, but his descent was hastened when his feet slipped from under him and he slid the rest of the way on his backside, feeling every step as he went down. Cold, wet and now bruised he returned to the house, and was quick to change into warm clothing and have a hot cup of tea. He could hardly hold the cup as his hand was still shaking. After gradually returning to some state of normality he stopped to look out the window. Outside he could see the children playing. Sharon had dressed them in warm coats, gloves and jelly bags.

"Look at me Daddy," yelled eight year old Pip, who had caught sight of Dad peering out the window. "This is fun, look at all the snow."

Suddenly six year old Harry came running around from the corner of the house snow ball in hand. With an evil glint in his eyes he was obviously up to no good. He launched his projectile in Pip's direction. It fell a metre in front of him and well out of range.

"You missed, you missed," taunted Pip.

Harry picked up some more snow.

"Why don't you children help Daddy make a snow man?" suggested Sharon.

"But . . . ," began Roger.

"Dear, the snows a treat. The children cannot have the snow without a snowman."

A SONG FOR COMMUNION

THE TWO BUSES, packed with 90 teenagers, were now well on their way to Invercargill, New Zealand's southernmost city.

"So, what are you doing at university, Sharon?" asked James.

"I'm majoring in English," replied Sharon. "I'm hoping to get into teaching overseas students English."

"Sounds cool," commented James.

"Do you like being in the Celebration Singers?" enquired Sharon.

"Yes, I have been in it almost since it started. Um . . . , about eight years."

"You must enjoy it then," stated Sharon.

"It's been great fun meeting other kids, doing concerts throughout New Zealand, and the television and recording stuff. It's been great . . . . and you?" asked James.

"I like gospel music and the mix of guitars, drums, an organ and other instruments. I'm certainly enjoying this concert tour and the people on it."

Sharon looked down and started fidgeting with the book she had brought to read. She hadn't had much opportunity, as there were so many people on the buses to get to know. At practices she had generally stuck with her friends and knew very little about other members in the choir.

The bus load of teenagers suddenly burst into song as a couple of teenagers led off and the rest joined in. After about four or five songs, the interest in singing waned and the teenagers returned to chatting and looking at the passing scenery.

The buses now passed through the picturesque town of Balclutha and crossed the mighty Clutha River. The deep blue of this river cutting its way through Balclutha was an incentive for some of the teenagers to quickly locate their cameras to capture the moment. The Clutha River is the South Island's longest river stretching for 150 miles from deep in the mountains to the east coast.

From Balclutha the buses continued through the rural landscape. The rich green paddocks of Southland certainly provided spectacular scenery. Dotted with white sheep, this was a reminder that the buses were entering Romney country. Romney comprise about half the 40million sheep in New Zealand, and were first introduced into New Zealand in 1843. They originated from the Romney Marshes in Kent, England.

It seemed paradoxical that the rich green land around the town of Gore was so profitable carrying large numbers of Romney, yet beneath this rich soil lay an equally valuable seam of coal, which could not be mined without first destroying the rich soil above.

"Gore," informed James; "home of the Romney."

The buses came to a stop.

"Must be a toilet stop," said Sharon. "It's only 11.05am; much too early to be a lunch stop."

The driver left the coach and joined the driver in the bus behind. Both drivers then returned and inspected the bus. They stood chatting for about five minutes, before returning to their buses.

"Sorry folks," said the driver, "we have a mechanical problem. It's going to take at least an hour to fix."

"The town's quite small, so if you want to go have a look around, or even to go to church (being a Sunday) then you can," added the choir conductor. "Just be back here by 12.30."

"There's a little Baptist church just up the road," suggested James, who had family in Gore.

Sharon and about 40 others decided to follow him up the road to the small church. James felt like he was leading a crusade when they entered the small church out-numbering the parishioners four to one.

Fortunately there were sufficient seats. Soon after entering the church, they observed one of the parishioners behind the altar frantically pouring communion wine into vessels. "Oh ye of little faith;" he had obviously not catered for a Christian revival. Following the final hymn and benediction the Minister rose to speak.

"I don't know who you are," he said, "but we are certainly glad to see you. Prior to our morning service our prayer group was praying for a bigger congregation. The Lord works in mysterious ways; hallelujah."

POT OF GOLD

"LOT OF STEAM coming from that shower room," yelled Jess.

"Having a Sauna," replied Charles jokingly.

"I've just been down to the road and there was a bit of an altercation."

"Sorry, can't hear you—soap in my ears," Charles shouted back.

"I'll wait till you get out of the shower," yelled Jess.

Five minutes later Charles emerged from the shower wrapped in a towel. "What's up?" he enquired.

"I was passing the old house before and there was a bit of an altercation going on between the owner and the demolition people. Apparently, they were taking stuff the neighbour had left in the house, when they had to evacuate."

"Sounds interesting, I might take a stroll down the drive," replied Charles, who liked to keep an ear to the ground.

Charles got dressed and strolled down the drive. He encountered the neighbour building up a pile of personal effects on the drive outside her entrance way.

"Just getting what we can out of the house before it is demolished next week," explained Zara the neighbour. "We had trouble with the demolition people taking stuff out of the house. But I guess, as we've been paid out, the stuff now belongs to the insurance company or the demolition company—whoever. Guess it really doesn't matter who. The demolition people said we could take our personal items like clothing."

"The stuff that has little value," commented Charles.

"You're on to it," replied Zara. "The good stuffs already been taken."

"It will be sad to see the old house demolished, though since the earthquakes it has been in a dilapidated state. Have you seen inside?" asked Zara.

"No, we've never been inside," replied Charles.

"Well, the inside has tasteful old wooden panelling, carved doors and hand-made lead windows. Upstairs in the main bedroom built into the wall is a beautiful Kauri set of drawers, a folding writing table and a cupboard—all in one. There is so much more I could tell you about. It's a shame all these beautiful things are going to be destroyed." Zara looked quite upset. "It was a wonderful house to live in, though it was very old."

"It is sad, this house was an icon," commented Charles with commiseration. "It was a grand old character home." Charles picked his moment, then left to continue walking down the drive.

On Monday morning Charles woke to an occasional crashing and shaking. He looked at his clock. It was only 7.40am—far too early for anyone in their right mind to be working.

"They're starting to demolish the old house," called out Jess, from the bathroom. Charles was a barrister who now worked from home, because his workplace had been damaged by the earthquake. Working from home enabled him to enjoy the comfort of bed for a bit longer in the mornings.

After Charles had finished his breakfast, he decided to investigate. He also needed to ensure that his prized Audi wouldn't be blocked in as he would need to use it later. He strolled down the drive edging his way past an old red Mitsubishi Galant parked near the entranceway to the old house. He assumed that this must belong to one of the workmen. A large, yellow bulldozer was at work demolishing one side of the house. Charles stood at the entranceway and observed the operation, as the large spade was pressed against a wall causing part of it to collapse. It wasn't long before he was approached by a man with an orange safety helmet.

"Do you live up the drive?" he asked.

"Yes," answered Charles.

"Just give me a yell if you need to get your car out."

"Thanks," replied Charles.

"You're not trying to recover the shingles off the roof?" asked Charles somewhat surprised as he watched the bulldozer shovel smash through the tiled roof.

"No, we are a demolition company; not a salvage company. Besides, the shingles will be no good. They split getting the nail out."

"Bloody shame," commented a heavily tattooed demolition man who had joined them. "About one hundred grands worth of shingles."

"$100,000 worth on this house?" repeated a surprised Charles.

"Yep," replied the tattooed man.

"A lot of nice woodwork in this house—a nice old wooden stairway," commented Charles looking towards part of the interior of the house, which had now become exposed following the bulldozers last push.

"Yes, a lot of nice things. But as I said we are a demolition company," restated the man in the orange helmet. "Besides there's no market for this sort of stuff—the markets already flooded."

"The earthquake has certainly been destructive, especially for those in the eastern suburbs," commented Charles.

"Bloody right," commented the tattooed man.

"Yeh," said another workman, who had joined the group.

"All right for youse in the ponsy areas, but us we have to wait weeks. Some of us still don't have water or a dunny."

"Bloody true," added the tattooed man.

"Yes, the eastern suburbs have been through a messy time especially with liquefaction, but for weeks after the first earthquake we too experienced difficulties like having to use our gardens for a toilet, and living off bottled water," interjected Charles.

"Ya didn't have all that flooding and mud through the house; though did ya now?" commented the workman.

"Some of us had to move out. Its bloody not easy finding a rental," added the tattooed man. "We got put up in one of these new temporary houses in the park."

"It certainly has been hard," agreed Charles. "But we also have had problems; a collapsed retaining wall, boulders smashing through houses, damaged foundations and so on," responded Charles. "Just a month ago we had raw sewerage pouring all over our lawn. Apparently, the pipe got damaged up the hill, and when they unblocked it the blockage moved down here."

"Where did it all go?" asked the man with the orange helmet.

"Over the cliff at the end of the property," replied Charles. "I guess we have the only house around here with a long drop."

The three workmen smirked.

"Hope nobody lives at the bottom of the cliff?" said the tattooed man lighting a cigarette.

"Yes, think his name is John," quipped Charles.

They all laughed.

"Ya still didn't get it like us," continued the workman. "Ya get shit over your lawn, the councils cleans it up. We have mud everywhere and are left with the mess."

Charles was quite annoyed because it was the people in the eastern suburbs making all the noises. It was as if nobody else got badly hit. Certainly, these people had been hit very hard and had to grin and bear it, probably longer than most, as many had nowhere else to go.

"Well I better not stop you from your work," Charles said judging this was an ideal time to move on. As a barrister he liked to debate, but sensed this was one he could lose. He was out numbered for starters.

Four days later Charles stopped to catch up on the progress. The old house had been removed and the bulldozer was now digging up foundations. Charles was soon joined by the man in the orange helmet.

"Remarkable!" exclaimed Charles. "The house has gone and now all that's left is a big empty section."

"Yes, we're almost finished, and you will have your drive back," replied the man in the helmet.

"Seems such a waste," sighed Charles. "All that lovely old stuff just dumped."

"Well, as I said before we are a demolition company not a salvage company," stated the man in the helmet.

"Then the pile of scrap metal," said Charles pointing to a high pile to one side of the excavation.

"Well er . . ."

"When you're in a hole you don't keep digging," quipped Charles.

"Sorry, what do you mean?" responded the man whose complexion was starting to look closer to his helmet colour.

"Oh, I was referring to the bulldozer over there in the foundation hole," Charles quickly replied. "Don't want to lose it."

"Right," replied the man. "No chance of that happening."

"Guess though, it's a pity nobody ever found the treasure," added Charles.

"Treasure? What treasure?"

"The old Spinster's gold sovereigns," replied Charles. "Apparently, the house was built over one hundred years ago for a wealthy spinster. In those days they didn't use banks. Instead they hid their money."

"Really, do you know where in the house?" asked the orange helmeted man.

"Not much point me telling you now with the house demolished and everything dumped," commented Charles.

"So where was it hidden?" asked the man in the orange helmet who was determined to get an answer.

"Ah, yes. It was thought that she had a secret compartment in a built in Kauri drawer structure. Nobody ever found the treasure though, and nobody will be able to find it now. The house and Kauri structure—all gone now."

"Did the structure have a writing desk?" enquired the man in the helmet.

"Yes," said Charles; "why?"

"Because I still have it."

CONGENIALITY

LINDSAY PEERED ACROSS at Trish. He had just finished watching his fifth movie on the plane and during most of this time Trish had been engrossed in a book. As an avid reader, she had taken advantage of the thirty hour trip from Christchurch to the UK. But now she had also stopped for another breather.

"What's wrong?" enquired Lindsay, as Trish was displaying those signs he had come to recognise as worry.

"I just hope this holiday with another couple works out," whispered Trish, as their friends Caroline and Jonathan Robinson were sitting just across the aisle.

"Why shouldn't it," responded Lindsay.

"Shush! You have a loud voice," snapped Trish.

"Look!" replied Lindsay in a quieter voice, "I have known Jono since we were teenagers. We dated girls together, went on holidays together, so why wouldn't this work out?"

"Ah, well you know dear, um . . . people change over time especially after they get married. As it is we are all different, and what we might want to do on the holiday may not be their cup of tea. You know they um . . . do mix in different circles dear."

Lindsay looked across at Jonathan who sat across the isle and had been glued to the cabin window. He hadn't changed. They still shared common interests. For a good part of the flight Jonathan had been intrigued by the aerial views of Europe, and occasionally he would excitedly shout across to Lindsay what he could see. Lindsay had no doubts that they would both get along just fine, and would get great enjoyment out of exploring the historical areas. Besides, there was so much to see like the Roman remains around Newcastle. In addition, just to the north of Newcastle, stretching across the hills and valleys, were the remains of Hadrian's Wall. The Roman emperor Hadrian had this built in 122AD to consolidate his boundaries keeping out the aggressive Scottish clans. Trish was wrong, as they would have a very good time together.

Soon the plane would be landing. Lindsay knew this from Jonathan's announcement; "Lindsay, the English Channel." The plane now started to veer to the right on a trajectory following the coast of England northwards towards Newcastle. Soon it would start its descent.

"No time for another movie," instructed Trish. "We should, thank goodness, be landing soon."

"Not watching another movie," replied Lindsay. "I'm just listening to some sympathy orchestra."

"Symphony orchestra," corrected Trish with a frown.

Shortly after, Lindsay, who liked to be organised, started to prepare for landing; first by disconnecting his headpiece, then by placing his reading glasses in the hand luggage he had stored under the seat. It wouldn't be long now.

With the plane having just landed, Trish now seemed somewhat happier. Those worry lines had disappeared. She hated travelling, though conversely relished the rare opportunity this provided to read. Caroline shared a similar sentiment though for different reasons. She detested being cooped up in the confinement of an aeroplane—a breeding ground for all sorts of nasty germs, and where there was little leg room. She had instructed Jonathan when they first got onto the plane to not turn on the air conditioning as she didn't want everyone else's bugs.

It was not surprising after such a long journey that all four were tired, but in good spirits having reached their destination.

"Shall I get a taxi?" asked Jonathan as they left the airport building.

"No need Jono," replied Lindsay. "The hotel is at the other side of this car park, just a short walk away."

"Brilliant!" complimented Jonathan.

"Glad we don't have more travel today," added Trish.

"As long as the hotel is not cheap and nasty," commented Caroline.

"Four star, Caroline," added Lindsay.

"Absolutely, I had every confidence you would do a great job in organising this trip," said a pleased Jonathan. "Just that Caroline is a bit fussy about where she stays."

At the hotel Lindsay pulled out his wallet.

"Do you take American Express?" he enquired. "If not I can pay cash."

"American Express will be fine," said the hotel receptionist.

Lindsay presented his card and signed the receipt.

Jonathan put his plastic card on the counter. He turned to Lindsay. "You really need to get a debit card. In these days people don't use credit cards when they travel. All you need is a debit card with a few thousand loaded on, plus a very small amount of money to cover the small expenditure like taxis and snacks."

"We don't normally use a credit card either," informed Trish.

"No, we are carrying mostly money. It beats having to pay ridiculous exchange rate fees," added Lindsay.

"You mean you're walking around with thousands of pounds on you waiting to be robbed?" asked an astonished Jonathan.

"Shush," interrupted Trish.

"Yes, but it is unlikely to happen," quietly replied Lindsay. "It's so much easier with money."

"You need to move out of the dark ages dear," commented Caroline. "Debit cards are the in thing."

Both couples found their rooms and agreed to meet the next morning for breakfast. That night after the discomfort of a long flight, they all slept very well.

The next morning Jonathan looked somewhat agitated.

"It's 8.15am and I'm starving. Where are they?"

"Darling, wearing out the floor won't make them come faster," commented Caroline. "Why don't you sit down, put your feet up and read the newspaper, or watch the news on the telly?"

"What's the point of travelling all this distance if people are going to spend half the morning in bed," said a grumpy Jonathan.

Jonathan resigned himself to reading the newspaper, while Caroline returned to reading her book.

About 9.00am there was a knock at the door. It was Lindsay.

"Good morning; did you both sleep well? It beats trying to sleep on the plane."

"Afternoon," responded Jonathan sarcastically. "So where's Trish?"

"Bathroom—still," replied Lindsay, slightly apologetically. "Should be here soon I guess. She's probably powdering her nose, or doing whatever woman do in bathrooms. Who cares; we're on holiday; relax."

Five minutes later Trish arrived, beautifully made up, and the four were ready to go down to breakfast.

"As we leave tomorrow for the Lake District, today we should go into town," suggested Lindsay.

"Definitely, shopping therapy; a nice way to start after all that travelling," replied Caroline. "A great suggestion."

"And of course there are areas of historical interest worthy of investigation," added an excited Jonathan.

"Like the castle," said Lindsay, who was equally excited.

"Great minds think alike," replied Jonathan. "Shall I get a taxi?" asked Jonathan.

"No need Jono," replied Lindsay. "All we need to do is walk back to the airport and all will be revealed."

They walked back to the airport and Lindsay asked them to follow him down a walkway at one end.

"Train at the doorstep and only £3 each," said a well satisfied Lindsay.

Jonathan looked at Caroline. Both did not look very enthralled.

"We would really prefer to take a taxi," commented Jonathan.

"You might ah, be looking at um . . . £30 to town, and you know how busy English roads can be. Would you want to spend the rest of the morning stuck in a traffic jam?" asked Trish.

Jonathan paused for a moment then agreed that the train might in this case be the best option. He had come to see England and not the back of a car. Caroline reluctantly succumbed to the group decision and hesitantly stepped onto the train. She scowled as she looked disapprovingly at the well worn seats on the train.

"Ook! I haven't been on public transport since I was at High School," complained Caroline. The seats and seating arrangement in particular reminded her of the school buses.

It became no easier for Caroline as the carriage began to fill from every stop on the way to Central Station. The prospect of picking up germs from the occasional sneeze, or cough added to her anxiety. Then there was the couple whose baby, periodically kept on crying over the 25minute trip. Towards the end of the journey she felt even more uncomfortable after a man of about 40 sat down in their carriage on one of the side seats and continued to stare in her direction. He was unshaven with long greasy hair, and wore an old trench coat reaching down to almost his ankles. Caroline felt quite out of place in the carriage, and was one of the first off the train when they arrived at Central Station.

"Great idea having light rail in the city," commented Lindsay. "It seems silly building more and more roads and parking buildings, when rail does the job."

"Interesting concept," replied Jonathan. "Though, who would want to travel on public transport?"

"Who; indeed?" added Caroline. "Quite disgusting."

They walked up the road to the shopping area. Town was busy, but not enough to make one feel agoraphobic. They stopped outside Sainsbury's, and decided to enter and investigate. Jonathan paused by the 1kg tins of Rose chocolates, but was dragged away by Caroline who reminded him that he had recently been diagnosed with diabetes.

"Look!" said Lindsay. The four turned in Lindsay's direction. "Free samples," he said pointing. Lindsay had spotted a woman giving away free food samples. Trish and Lindsay excitedly walked over to get a free tasting. The Robinsons however, went off disapprovingly, in the opposite direction.

After the couples had reunited, Caroline suggested that the boys might like to go and see the castle while they the girls did a spot of shopping. Trish was very much in agreement. Having Lindsay around her feet, especially when shopping for women's clothing, cramped her style. The boys on the other hand were keen to explore and were more than happy to leave their wives shopping. They set off towards the River Tyne over which the castle takes a commanding position.

Lindsay soon realised that Jonathan was struggling to keep up.

"Jono, going to Uni and getting a cushy office job hasn't done your health much good," taunted Lindsay. "You should have done a trade like me."

"Have to say, you have done well for yourself in the building industry, despite dropping out of school," said Jonathan catching his breath. Jonathan was no longer the slim lad Lindsay had known. He was now a plump unfit 45 year-old. They continued to walk down the road, but at a slower pace. Finally they reached the castle. By this stage Jonathan was well out of breath.

"Wow!" exclaimed Lindsay. "Neat castle, I can even see the remains of the moat."

"Not a castle," corrected Jonathan who had got his breath back. "It's in fact a Keep, which is a fortified tower. It was built on an old fortified Roman site by Henry II and improved on by King John."

"Gee, you certainly know your stuff," commented an impressed Lindsay.

Lindsay followed Jonathan who slowly ascended the steep stone steps into the Keep. They paid for tickets and explored the lower level where there was a museum. After looking at the collection of swords and armour they climbed up the windy stairway to the four turrets.

From one of these towers they had a panoramic view of the Tyne River and Newcastle.

"That was something," said Lindsay. "To think this Keep is almost one thousand years old."

"Yes, it certainly did keep," said Jonathan jokingly, "and is in pristine condition. Look, you can see the remains of the surrounding walls that were once part of this fortification."

The two walked down the hill to the river to where they were meeting their wives.

"Glad we came on this trip together," said Jonathan. "It's like old times, even if you are looking rather older and balder now."

"Yep," replied Lindsay, "That's what age does to you."

The girls were waiting down by the Millennium Bridge.

"Did you have a good time shopping?" asked Jonathan.

"Great, darling," replied Caroline. "Though Trish wanted me to go into this charity shop. Ook! There is no way I am buying second-hand stuff."

"It's not um all second-hand stuff," interrupted Trish. A lot of the labelled names donate new clothing to support these charities. Ah, you can find a lot of top quality clothing in these stores. Besides it is helping these charities. Anyhow, while I was there I donated the book I had finished reading."

"Well you won't find me going in there," replied Caroline.

After having a good look around the river area and visiting the convention centre (nick-named The Slug), the couples decided to part company for the rest of the day.

The next morning they met for breakfast and picked up the rental car for their six days around the Lake District.

"You've done well Lindsay dear," complemented Caroline. "A VW Golf is a good choice of car."

"Superb," confirmed Jonathan. "You can't beat European for class."

"Good mileage to the gallon too," said Lindsay. "It runs on diesel."

"Diesel!" exclaimed Caroline, who looked quite shocked. "A VW on diesel? Diesel is for tractors. No, you've got to be mistaken."

"I'm sure you will enjoy the car ride, Caroline," reassured Jonathan. They now were heading towards Hadrians Wall with Jonathan navigating.

"Hope you don't mind," said Jonathan, "but I am directing you to a car park where we just need to hop out to see the wall. There is a track further up the road, but I don't think we have time for a long walk. Besides you might have to pay," he added sarcastically. From the car park they could see the stone wall stretching across the hills and valleys. It was no more than 2 metres high.

"Disappointing," commented Jonathan. "The wall was originally much higher and had watch-towers and gates. At this height they would not have stopped the Caledonians."

"Caledonians?" questioned Lindsay.

"The name given to the Scottish clans at that time," replied Jonathan.

"Well, where are we off to now?" asked Trish.

"A place called Pooley Bridge on Lake Ullswater," replied Lindsay. "We are staying in an old pub which dates back to the 1700s, I think."

"Pub!" commented a disapproving Caroline.

"Excellent, 1700s, great!" exclaimed Jonathan.

During their stay at Lake Ullswater the couples enjoyed the views of the lake and the generous English breakfast provided at the pub. Only one of the four was disapproving of the accommodation, and that was because she preferred modern four star hotels.

The remaining nights were spent around the other lakes in the towns of Kendal, Keswick, and Ambleside. Bed and breakfast accommodation was a first and last experience for both Jonathan and Caroline. It was simply not four star accommodation, as far as Caroline was concerned. For Jonathan the problem lay with moving his body weight and bags up steps to bedrooms. In England people live on smaller areas of land—hence mostly in multi-storey dwellings with the bedrooms upstairs.

The women in particular were thrilled to visit the Beatrix Potter museum at Windemere, and see the birth place of William Wordsworth at Cockermouth. Lindsay and Jonathan also enjoyed the small township of Windemere built on the hillside and looking out across the vast blue lake. It was a beautiful spot though ruined by its popularity. One had to even queue to get an ice cream.

Hotel at Pooley Bridge

This was their last day around the lakes. It would be a shame to leave this beautiful area. They had seen such wonderful scenery and had shared some good times together. Tomorrow they would head back to Newcastle where the couples would part company for just over a week. Lindsay and Trish were training down to Nottingham to spend time with Trish's relatives, while the Robinsons were heading up to Scotland and joining a Coach tour. They would meet again for several days in Newcastle before returning to New Zealand.

Time passes quickly when you're on holiday, and soon Trish and Lindsay had caught up with relatives in Nottingham, and the Robinsons had explored Scotland.

On returning to the hotel in Newcastle, Trish and Lindsay were given a message at the reception desk which had been left by the Robinsons.

"They have just dropped a note to say they have gone into town."

"On a taxi!" added Lindsay.

"Presumably," continued Trish finding the comment amusing. "Anyhow they said they would catch up with us tomorrow for the rugby."

"Oh yes, it would be a crime for any Kiwi to miss the footy, especially being the world cup match between New Zealand and Aus," added Lindsay.

Lindsay was up bright and early the next morning to join Jonathan in front of the television. Trish and Caroline left the boys to enjoy a beer and watch the rugby.

"Australia will win," teased Caroline going out the door.

"No chance of that," responded Lindsay taking the bait. "Beating them will be a piece of cake."

Caroline laughed, and the two women went downstairs for breakfast. When the girls returned it was half time.

"Well, is Australia winning?" taunted Trish, trying to take off from where Caroline had left.

"They would like to be, but are just not good enough," replied Jonathan. "Australia may be there in four years time, but now they are still at the team rebuilding stage."

The women went off to the other room and left their husbands to watch the football. Forty minutes later the men came bursting through the door in a jovial mood.

"Right we need to get food," stated Jonathan.

"I take it we won then," said Trish.

"Affirmative; never any suggestion we wouldn't," replied Jonathan, "but now we need to eat."

"You can get breakfast in town Lindsay," said Trish. Then leaning towards Lindsay she whispered: "Caroline um offered to take us in their taxi. It's not costing us anything, so we might as well go with them."

"OK," replied Lindsay. "But with five of us in a taxi we will be packed like a tin of salmon."

"Sardines," corrected Trish giving Lindsay an odd look.

They set off in the taxi for town. When they arrived they decided to split up as each couple had plans for their last day. Both had in mind buying a few gifts for their families. It was also a last chance to take in the sights of Newcastle. Jonathan had told Lindsay about the 1300 AD remains of the old fortified town wall down by China Town. This was something Lindsay had to see.

Lindsay and Trish had a great time finding gifts for their family. They also found some charity shops and some bargains. As they had arranged to meet up with the Robinsons after tea, they found a carvery called "The Goose", and had an enjoyable meal. Now feeling well fed they set off to where they had arranged to meet. The Robinsons were already there.

"Have you dined?" enquired Jonathan. "We have. Caroline found this quaint Italian restaurant and we had just enough left on our debit card to have a very tasty pepperoni," he added.

"Yes, we have eaten too. Found a pub . . ."

"A pub!" interrupted Caroline somewhat disgusted.

"Yes, it was only £3 something for a carvery," added Lindsay.

"Cheep and nasty," commented Caroline. "You might get food poisoning and be unable to fly home tomorrow. Lindsay dear, you need to splash out and buy quality food."

"I guess that it isn't everyone's cup of tea. It was only cuttings of turkey, beef, and ham with mashed potato, peas, carrots, leaks, gravy,and various dressings; that's all," Lindsay replied sarcastically.

Jonathan smacked his lips and looked rather envious. It sounded much more appetising than his pepperoni.

"Oh! By the way Jono, I got a new shirt," Lindsay said as he produced a shirt still in its packet.

"Very nice, I am impressed—a Marks and Spencer. Your taste is improving. That must have knocked you back about £50 or £60," commented Jonathan, who was looking for something in his wallet.

"No! Got it from the charity shop for £10," replied Lindsay.

"Then it has got to be a second dear," commented Caroline.

"Well guess it must be time to go back to the Hotel," said Trish intervening before the holiday ended in blood being spilt. Jonathan nodded as he put his wallet back into his pocket. He whispered something to Caroline, who then searched through her bag and shook her head.

"Are you going back by taxi?" asked Lindsay, hopeful of a free ride back being on offer. He had now developed a taste for the comfort of a taxi compared to the hard seats of the train. Besides, the train was rather crowded, and it seemed like everyone tended to be staring at one another. Perhaps Caroline did have a point. Yes, he rather fancied the comfort of a taxi as long as he wasn't paying.

"Well! Er, we were going to suggest we take the train back to the hotel," said Jonathan.

NOTTINGHAM ADVENTURE

THE TRAIN PULLED into Newark station.

"This is where we get off," advised Trish.

Waiting at the station was Aunt Dot, a short, thin, grey-headed lady, who had puffed her way through quite a few thousand cigarettes over a life-time. This was somewhat evident in her appearance. Trish gave her aunt a big hug, before the three made their way to Aunt Dot's small car.

Both Trish and Lindsay gagged on the cigarette smell which greeted them on entering the vehicle.

"Is it very far to Nottingham?" asked Lindsay, hoping he didn't have to put up with this smell for too long.

"A fair way love," replied Aunt Dot, "But ya will enjoy the ride. We pass Sherwood Forest. Ya may even see some red deer. Did ya have a comfy ride in the train dear?" she asked Trish.

"It was very comfortable."

". . . and fast," added Lindsay.

"I um think even Caroline would have approved of the comfortable seating," commented Trish.

"Caroline?" enquired Dot.

"Sorry, Caroline and Jonathan are the couple we travelled with around the Lake District," explained Trish.

"Caroline's a bit of a snob," added Lindsay.

"You can't say that," said Trish. "She is really nice, when you get to know her."

"What's that over there?" asked Lindsay pointing towards an old derelict castle.

"Oh, that's Newark castle. Don't know much about it," replied Aunt Dot. "History is not my thing. Would ya like to stop here and see the ruins?"

"Yes please," said Lindsay and Trish, both at the same time. It was a good chance to get some fresh air. Lindsay was also keen to see the castle and compare it to the Keep he had visited in Newcastle.

"This is where Jono would have been useful," whispered Lindsay to Trish. "He would have been able to give us the history of these ruins."

Newark Castle

Later Lindsay was able to ask Jonathan about the castle. He learned from Jonathan that this was where King John died. There was also some colourful history relating to the War of the Roses.

They explored the ruins, and took some deep breaths of fresh air to help them through the remainder of the journey to Arnold, a suburb of Nottingham.

Aunt Dot's house in Arnold was even more polluted than the car. Her years of smoking had resulted in the smell permeating the walls, drapes, carpet and furnishings. Both Lindsay and Trish tried to put on brave faces while quietly choking on the acrid smell.

"Change of plans. I would have put ya up, but my friend Lorna is down from Blackpool. You'll meet her tomorrow. Hope ya don't mind, but Sarah and Hugh offered to have ya stay while ya here in Nottingham. They don't live very far away."

"We are very grateful," replied Trish.

"Yes," said Lindsay breathing a sigh of relief.

Aunt Dot made some lunch then they left in her car.

Sarah and Hugh lived in a semi-detached house, identical to every other house on the street. When they arrived Sarah greeted Trish with a hug and kiss on both sides of her cheeks then similarly hugged and kissed Lindsay.

"Are you alright?" she asked Lindsay.

"I think so," said Lindsay, though somewhat concerned his exposure to cigarette pollution may have had some detrimental effect. Did he really look that bad?

"Sorry dear, I should have told you that in England this is a standard greeting," informed Trish. Both Trish and Sarah laughed. "It's a bit like us greeting people with 'how are you'?"

Sarah showed them upstairs to their bedroom, then Lindsay returned to get the cases. He rejoined the women shortly after in the kitchen. They were having a good old chat.

"Here, we brought you a bottle of New Zealand wine," said Lindsay.

"Thank you," replied Sarah. "We can have this with our meal. I don't know if Mum told you on the way here, but I am not a very good cook. We usually purchase ready made meals from Sainsbury's. Hope you don't mind."

"I'm sure they will be tasty," replied Trish.

Later Hugh arrived home from work. Shaking Lindsay's hand he asked, "Are you alright?"

"Good," replied Lindsay. "We had a comfortable train ride down from Newcastle and I love what I have seen of England so far."

"You would find England quite cheap with your improved exchange rate," commented Hugh.

"Oh, I should have told you that Hugh teaches economics," interrupted Sarah.

"Not an area I know much about," replied Lindsay. "Only had a high school education. I do know that it takes two of our dollars to make up one of your pounds, which makes England expensive."

"Yes, but your average salary is twice ours, which tends to balance out this difference," responded Hugh. "Our problem in England is that our standard of living is falling as we waste time trying to bail out the Greeks who think the world owes them a living."

"Not the Greeks again love," interrupted Sarah. "Our guests don't want to hear about the Greeks."

"Well they should be kicked out of the EEC," responded Hugh getting quite worked up.

The next day Trish and Lindsay caught a bus into the central business area of Nottingham. They had a good time exploring the area, shops, and Goose Fair, before returning. That night they got to meet some of Trish's relatives. It was evident that Aunt Dot had been busy organising their Nottingham week.

"Now tomorrow evening ya cuz Henry and Gwen wanted to take ya out to a restaurant," advised Aunt Dot. "They will come here half six to pick ya up. Ah, this is my friend Lorna," she added, as an elderly lady in her mid-seventies joined them.

Lorna gave them both a hug then looking at Lindsay asked, "Are ya a Maori?"

"No," replied Lindsay.

"Oh," I thought ya was love, since ya live in New Zealand," she explained. "Do ya find England modern?" she asked.

"Sorry . . . , modern? Not at all. New Zealand is in many ways more modern," replied Lindsay to a somewhat surprised Lorna.

"Lorna has never been outside of England," explained Aunt Dot quietly to Lindsay.

Lindsay took the first opportunity available and left Lorna with Aunt Dot. He joined Trish who was talking to other relatives.

"This is my Uncle Michael," said Trish. Lindsay shook his hand. "He and Aunt Martha are having us around one night for a meal. Uncle Michael is an exceptionally good pianist and said he will play us some pieces."

"Can't wait," replied Lindsay. "I did enjoy listening to that orchestra on the plane."

Trish then took Lindsay around to meet all the other relatives. "Apparently on the last night we are all meeting together again but in some pub for a meal."

"Sounds great," replied Lindsay. "We haven't had many pub meals in England. I certainly will be looking forward to that."

The next day was spent sight seeing around Nottingham. They walked up the hill, around the walls of Nottingham castle, and entered through the gate into the castle gardens.

"Looks like um . . . you have to pay to go any further," said Trish.

"I'm not fussed," replied Lindsay. "Jono said some Duke built his mansion on the castle site. I'm not paying just to see his mansion." They walked back out the entrance and down the hill.

"Ah there's the statue of Robin Hood," said Trish pointing towards a lawn near the high castle walls. They walked further down the road. "Here is the oldest Inn in England," said Trish as they came around the corner of the wall. They continued to walk around completing a circuit of the castle.

That night Henry and Gwen arrived in semi-formal dress to take them out for a meal. Lindsay felt a bit out of place in his jeans and tee shirt. Trish had forgot to mention to Lindsay that they were both lawyers and quite wealthy.

"Didn't realise we were going somewhere flash," he whispered to Trish. Henry passed Lindsay and Trish a menu. Lindsay's mouth dropped when he saw the prices.

"Will you be having soup and an entrée?" asked Henry.

"I am really not that hungry. I think I will just stick to the main," replied Lindsay.

"So will I, I'm not a big eater," said Trish.

Trish had a great time catching up with her cousin during the meal and they made plans to meet again.

Once home Lindsay breathed a sigh of relief. "That was an expensive night," he declared.

"Lindsay, Gwen and Henry have offered to take us out later in the week to another restaurant," said Trish. Lindsay cringed and his hand reached into his pocket to feel the number of fifty pound notes left. Tonight had taken two. Now there was another expensive restaurant planned. It didn't leave them with much money for Newcastle. Lindsay prided himself on his organisational skills and he thought he had been generous with their cash budget. He didn't want to resort to using the credit card and paying hefty exchange rate fees.

"You'll um be fine," reassured Trish. "Apart from the hotel, we haven't needed to use the credit card yet. It was really a nice meal, and besides we are on holiday," said Trish.

"I didn't think so," replied Lindsay. "All that money for a big white plate with an uncooked fillet steak in the centre, a spoonful of vegetables on one side and some blobs of sauce sprinkled on the other. I went there to eat; to have a fulfilling meal. If I had wanted to see artwork I would have gone to an art gallery."

"The meat's meant to be a little red," commented Trish. "It should be tender, not overcooked and tough. It was really a lovely meal."

"Well red meat is not everyone's cup of coffee."

"Tea," corrected Trish, shaking her head.

"Besides meat can be brown and still melt in your mouth, but it takes a good cook like my mum. Her steaks were brown and perfect."

"Yes she was exceptional," responded Trish.

The remaining days passed quickly and as suspected Gwen and Henry had chosen to take them to another artwork exhibition featuring ways of decorating a plate with small items of food. After this big spend-up, Lindsay could now only feel one fifty pound note in his wallet. Tomorrow they would be on the train heading back for Newcastle where they would have one day before returning to New Zealand. It would be nice to have some money left to buy something for their family. Tonight they were dining at a pub with all the relatives. Being a pub this shouldn't break the bank.

"Should be a really nice meal tonight," said Sarah. "Mum said that Gwen and Henry have chosen the venue, and they really know their food."

"It's alright dear," reassured Trish, "um . . . ,there is always the credit card."

The pub was indeed upmarket and all the relatives were there. Trish and Lindsay felt so honoured by their presence. They had been so helpful with meals and transport and had made Trish and Lindsay feel so welcome.

"Now what are you going to have?" asked Hugh planting the menu under Lindsay's nose. "You must start with a soup."

Lindsay looked at the menu. Although the prices were less than Gwen and Henry's fancy restaurants, these were still much higher than normal pub prices. Once again a main would suffice.

"I'll just have this porterhouse steak main," decided Lindsay, passing the menu to Trish.

"And I will have the chicken dish," said Trish.

"No, you need some soup first," insisted Hugh, and before they could say a further word, soup had been ordered.

After the main Lindsay started to tally the cost in his head. Having to use his credit card now seemed a real possibility.

"Now you must have dessert," commented Hugh.

"No really," said both Lindsay and Trish, "we are quite full."

"Yes, you must," said Gwen. "This place is famous for its desserts. You can come here and not have a soup or a main, but you must have a dessert."

"Alright then," said Trish, looking through the menu. Lindsay, now in a hot sweat also agreed. Things were outside his control. It was apparent their budget would be blown.

"Definitely now the credit card," whispered Trish. Lindsay sadly nodded in agreement.

The dessert went down very favourably and both Trish and Lindsay agreed to finish the meal with a coffee. It really didn't matter now. Lindsay reached deep down into his wallet to find the credit card.

"Well I guess we had better pay our bill," he said.

"No need," said Aunt Dot, "you have come all this way from New Zealand. We are paying."

SCOTTISH WHIRL

"SORRY DEAR, BUT this hotel has no vacancies either," stated Jonathan. "I think we may need to consider a more expensive hotel. All the four star hotels seem to have been taken. There must be some big attraction on in Edinburgh at the moment."

"Probably a soccer match," commented Caroline. "This sort of thing tends to happen in the UK. I just wish that you were more organised like Lindsay. If you had booked before we left for the UK, we would have now had somewhere to stay."

Caroline and Jonathan had just spent the last week travelling around the Lake District with their friends Trish and Lindsay. They were now looking forward to the second part to their holiday—a coach tour of Scotland. Tomorrow they would explore Edinburgh. Their coach tour commenced the following day. Meanwhile they needed to find a hotel for their two nights in Edinburgh.

Finally Jonathan found a hotel with a spare room, though this was a much more expensive hotel than what they had planned. They weren't too worried though. As Caroline had often said, "when you're overseas you forget about things like exchange rates and enjoy yourselves." In fact, Caroline was more than happy with the more up market accommodation. It was quite a change from Lindsay's choice of accommodation; something she had never warmed to.

Shopping the Royal Mile also met with her satisfaction, whereas Jonathan was more interested in exploring Edinburgh Castle. So, while

Caroline indulged in some retail therapy the next day and also looked for a Campbell tartan—being her clan, Jonathan walked the Royal Mile to Edinburgh castle. The castle was in pristine condition; perched on a rocky outcrop the location provided a near impregnable defence. From the Argyle Battery Jonathan had a commanding view to the North and could see the Firth of Forth. He was most taken by Mons Meg, a 550 year-old cannon. Despite its age, it had the firepower to send a gun-stone almost two miles.

The next morning they boarded the coach. In the brochure the description had sounded quite up market with things like air conditioning, stereo sound system, adjustable high backed seats and many other features. But in reality while the high back seats and air conditioning provided for comfort, the thought of being compacted into one vehicle with 30 plus other people, to Caroline was claustrophobic. The type of people in the coach was also not what she had envisaged. When her parents had been on a coach trip about thirty years ago, the passengers were mostly American and Canadian, and of a similar age. On this coach there were no other New Zealanders, and apart from about six much older couples, the remaining passengers were much younger and of Asian ethnicity.

Jonathan, conversely, found the experience exciting. Scotland had a lot of history: the Caledonians, William Wallace, Bonnie Prince Charlie, Mary Queen of Scots, and other historical people and areas of interest. He couldn't wait for the coach to start off on the journey north.

Things looked promising as the driver had now settled down on his seat and the tour guide had picked up the microphone.

"Good evening folks; my name is Geoff, and I'm your tour guide. Today we are passing through the famous town of St Andrews known for golf. Unfortunately, we won't have enough time to stop at the nineteenth hole. On this stretch of the journey we will also stop on the Culloden Moors. Here you will be able to see where Bonnie Prince Charlie took his last stand against the English Redcoats. We will then continue on to Inverness where we will spend two nights."

Jonathan couldn't wait to see Culloden where Charles ignored his General's advice by deciding to stand his ground against the English. Had he continued to retreat and drawn George II Redcoats into the depths of the highlands, then Scottish and English history may have been significantly different. Instead, Charlie attacked and was heavily defeated losing 1500 to 2000 men. Following the battle the Duke of Cumberland, commander of the Redcoats, sobriquet 'the butcher', ruthlessly had survivors hunted down and killed.

At Culloden, Jonathan walked through the battle ground and studied the position of each Scottish clan before stopping at those of his ancestors. The wife of one of his ancestors had found her husband lying amongst the dead following the battle. To avoid capture, he was hidden, then he later escaped to Ireland where he changed his name. Jonathan was so engrossed in the battle field and positioning of the clans that he was late returning to the coach. He was not given a warm reception, on entering the bus, by his fellow travellers.

"I hate public transport darling," commented Caroline. "People can be so horrible. You were only seven minutes late getting back."

The coach continued on its way to Inverness where they were to stay two nights. Tomorrow they would travel to the Isle of Skye. On arriving at Inverness, they took their bags to the hotel room then joined the other travellers for a hearty Scottish meal before retreating to their room. They had no interest in socialising with the other passengers in the bar.

After two nights stay in Inverness both Caroline and Jonathan were ready to move on through the highlands.

"Loch Ness," announced the tour guide. "Can you spot the monster?" Cameras came out to take a picture of one big lake minus a monster. Jonathan couldn't be bothered with fictitious monsters. It was just another lake. The coach continued on towards Fort William.

"We spend two nights at Fort Williams," announced Geoff. "Now tomorrow, for those who are interested we will be taking the coach to Ben Nevis."

"Are you interested?" asked Caroline.

"No, might be Britain's biggest mountain, but it would be just a hill in New Zealand," replied Jonathan.

"I'm not interested either," replied Caroline. "I would rather explore Fort Williams and its shops. Besides I am getting rather tired of being cooped up in the coach for most of each day. I will welcome the break."

Instead of going to Ben Nevis, the next day they walked down the steps from their hotel to the shopping area below. Caroline and Jonathan found Fort Williams very appealing. Caroline found some good souvenirs to take home including her coat of arms. They were also able to go for some nice walks.

"Well, tomorrow is the final day, so how have you found this tour of Scotland?" asked Jonathan.

"Where do I start darling?" said Caroline. "Firstly, the hotels we have stayed in are tolerable, but the food lacks imagination; there is no presentation; just a plateful of food. Secondly, I hate trains, buses and public transport of any type. I am looking forward to us driving back to Newcastle. I have enjoyed the scenery, but next time I think we should hire a car. How have you found it?"

"Loved every minute," replied Jonathan. "It was great catching up on my ancestry and seeing historical sites. I guess you must have also enjoyed finding some of your ancestry: the tartan and coat of arms," he added.

The bus left early the next day for Glasgow. They were winding through the hills through rugged landscape when the tour guide picked up the microphone.

"This place is called Glen Coe, the home of the MacDonald," he announced. "Four hundred years ago the Campbell clan visited the MacDonalds who were very hospitable and let them stay as guests. One night, the Campbells slew the MacDonalds while they were asleep. Four hundred years on, the MacDonalds have never forgotten and no Campbell is welcome here. Just hope there are no Campbells on the bus, as this stretch of road is notorious for buses experiencing mechanical problems," he added looking in Caroline's direction.

"Bit of a worry," said Jonathan smirking.

THE END IN SIGHT

IT WAS NOW just over one year from the February earthquake which destroyed the New Zealand city of Christchurch. The earthquake of 6.3 Richter scale had been destructive with half the central business areas buildings damaged to the extent of requiring demolition. It was calculated that the force was the equivalent of 49,000 tonnes of TNT exploding. From the seismic activity over Christchurch, liquefaction had resulted in 580,000 tonnes of silt being deposited over roads, properties and even through floors of houses. Due to sewerage pipes being damaged, 2000 portaloos and 40,000 chemical toilets had been supplied to affected citizens until these services could be restored. As for Alex and Bruce, they had now been relegated from a central city location to a small office in an industrial area. Like so many other central city workers, they had relocated to safe buildings in the suburbs until their building had been cleared as safe to reoccupy.

Alex and Bruce sat on the balcony eating their lunch. It was much nicer soaking in the summer sunshine outside than enduring the cool air conditioning within the office. Alex bit into a ham sandwich, while Bruce peeled a banana.

"Well, a lot has happened since February 22nd last year," commented Bruce. "It is so frustrating being stuck out here with no banks, no shops. I would just like to get back into our building and town."

"What matters is that we are safe," said Alex. "Besides, we've never had it better with free car parking within a stone's throw."

"That's true," replied Bruce. "Tell me, I've been meaning to ask you; how do you feel now having removed dead bodies from the collapsed CTV building? Has that affected you in any way; like do you think about it often? Can you sleep at night?"

"No, I'm good," replied Alex. "Though I know what you're getting at. Experiences like this can be traumatic for some people and can affect their sleep, work; everything."

"Some days I have feelings of guilt," responded Bruce. "I half thought about returning to town to help those who might be injured or buried, but like many others did nothing. I guess the reality of the situation didn't fully register at the time."

"I think you did the right thing going home and ensuring that your family was safe," reassured Alex. "You know the rescuing thing is not for everyone. The police have some training for these types of situations and I have training in civil defence. There is no need to feel guilty." Alex pulled out a Boston bun from his lunch bag and took a bite.

"Well you're an unsung hero," stated Bruce, putting down his coffee mug beside his seat "You know it's really true what a man wrote in the newspaper."

"What was that?" asked Alex.

"He was really miffed that many of those who had slaved away on the day rescuing others and retrieving bodies had gone unrecognised; yet others who did very little were quick to claim the credit."

"Isn't that human nature?" Alex asked, as he was chewing on his bun. "Besides, there is no I in teamwork."

Bruce grunted in agreement, as he picked up his mug to have another sip. "You know he was not the only one miffed. There has been a lot of heated debate over the future of the Cathedral and preservation of heritage buildings. On TV it was also reported that business owners have been complaining, and are upset at the lack of consultation and not having access to their business premises. Some have even learned that their buildings have been demolished. There's an irony that they can ban these people and Christchurch citizens from the cordoned areas yet allow celebrities access. Whose city is it?

"Well, after what Christchurch has been through, we are all scratchy," replied Alex. "It has certainly been a very trying time and after each large aftershock, more buildings become destabilised and more have to be demolished. It is never ending. Allowing people to access their buildings comes at a risk which the authorities are wisely reluctant to take. On the whole, those sorting out the various issues have handled things very well. I agree that there have been problems. Especially the looters, burglars masquerading as damage assessors, and some unscrupulous people in business who have been overcharging."

"My uncle used to say that when you bring things to the boil scum rises to the top," said Bruce.

"That's true," replied Alex. "There are always some who want to benefit from the misfortunes of others."

"Or seek to profit from the situation," added Bruce. "Thank goodness it's almost all over now and we can return to some normality. The Greendale fault line, which started everything off seventeen months ago, now seems to have finally settled. The February and June Port Hill fault lines seems to have also stabilised."

"But the December fault line out to sea is still now and again declaring its presence," added Alex. "Is it really all over?"

"True, though for the last three weeks it has been quiet with no aftershocks," replied Bruce. "I think that by now if there are anymore fault lines poised to pop, they would already have gone with all the shaking."

Alex shook his head. "The calm before the storm; don't you remember? Last year we thought it was all over after the shaking ceased for about two or three weeks. Then on February 22nd at 12.51pm, Christchurch shook to pieces—another fault line discovered, but this time under the Port Hills. Since then we have twice experienced calm periods only for these to be broken by the June and December Richter scale 6 earthquakes. How can you be so sure it's all over? The whole thing's a continuing nightmare."

"Well, this time it is different," replied Bruce. "By now the fault-lines would have expended all their energy. What was going to shake has shaken, and what was going to fall down has fallen down. The tectonic plates probably won't move now for another three hundred years. It's time to move on and for people to not be so paranoid; to rebuild the city and replace skyscrapers with skyscrapers. Let's just get on with life instead of fluffing about and erring on the side of caution. Calm before the storm; utter rubbish. Yay! We've reached the end." Bruce suddenly lurched forward grabbing the balcony rails.

"It was only a big truck passing," said Alex laughing.

HOPE

Life is full of ups and downs
Of smiles and laughter, tears and frowns.
These are the days and nights of life
The pleasure, ease, down-time and strife.

Life is not fair, we're not born equal
We are who we are, there is no sequel.
Things about ourselves we do not like
Dwelled on will haunt us all our life.

The moments of life are a treasure,
Find the sunshine in bad weather.
And in those times we strive to cope
Remember there is always hope

Brian Wilson

Make the Most of Every Moment

AUTHORS BIOGRAPHY

AS A LONG-TIME friend of Brian and his wife Karen, I felt privileged when asked to write this Author's Biography. Our friendship extends back to primary school days and over the years that followed when we enjoyed tramping (hiking) in the beautiful South Island bush of New Zealand. I'm glad that as you read this book of Brian's, you will share in the delight of wit and emotion—of people in situations in which you might see yourself and also feel the emotion and humour.

Brian is a caring person and on one occasion he spent 6 weeks in voluntary service at a missionary hospital in Zambia. He also likes to encourage others to step out of their comfort zone. After he completed a Masters Degree in Psychology, I was motivated to complete a Masters Degree in Professional Studies. Brian has accounting and management qualifications as well.

As a family man who loves music and sport, he has enjoyed seeing his wife and 3 adult children develop a similar passion.

Brian loves to be known as an average Kiwi bloke. He writes his stories with the hope that the reader will get enjoyment and inspiration. I know that you will.

David Moore